www.SaucyRomanceBooks.com/RomanceBooks

Forgotten Love

Her memory lost, a baby on the way...

Brought to you by best selling author Cher Etan.

The story of childhood sweethearts Allen and Frances, and a moment that changes their lives forever.

After a brutal accident leaves Frances hospitalized, doctors soon discover she has amnesia.

With no recollection of who she or Allen is, the doctors go to work on helping her recover.

But as they do, a shocking truth is discovered; Frances is pregnant!

A surprise to them both, now she must live in a house she has no memory of and a husband she can't remember.

Can Frances regain her memory, rekindle forgotten love, and prepare to care for her unborn baby?

Find out in this emotional yet sexy romance by best selling author Cher Etan.

Suitable for over 18s only due to sex scenes so hot, you'll need a fireman on stand by.

Get Free Romance eBooks!

Hi there. As a special thank you for buying this book, for a limited time I want to send you some great ebooks completely **free of charge** directly to your email! You can get it by going to this page:

www.saucyromancebooks.com/physical

You can see a the cover of these books on the next page:

ONE LONE COWBOY, ONE WOMAN ON A MISSION...
THE LONE COWBOY
EMILY
ROCHELLE
IF IT'S MEANT TO BE...
Him
KIMBERLY GREENFORD
PLAYERS GONNA PLAY?
SHE'S THE ONE HE WANTS BUT CAN SHE TRUST HIM?
ONE VAMPIRE. ONE COP. ONE LOVE.
VAMPIRES OF CLEARVIEW
J A FIELDING

www.SaucyRomanceBooks.com/RomanceBooks

These ebooks are so exclusive you can't even buy them.

When you download them I'll also send you updates when new books like this are available.

Again, that link is:

www.saucyromancebooks.com/physical

ISBN-13: 978-1515247012

ISBN-10: 1515247015

Contents

Chapter 1

"You want to leave me over some bullshit like this? Okay then, go! Leave!" Frances began pushing Allen until his legs were outside the door. Then she collapsed on the floor and cried until she had no more tears. She didn't expect that he would try to come back. He was about as mad as she was. It wasn't her fault; she was trying her best. She couldn't *help* the fact that her book had suddenly blown up; that she was now as busy as he was. It wasn't her fault they didn't get to spend as much time as they used to together. The problem with Allen St. James is that he was spoiled; being the man with the money meant that he didn't have to wait his turn for everything. He was always ushered to the front of the line, always the one who kept people waiting. She'd stood by his side these ten years, ever since they were two teenage kids who found themselves on the street with no one to rely on but each other. Allen's parents had been killed in a plane crash coming back from the island of St. Maarten where they'd been celebrating their twenty year anniversary. Fourteen year old Allen had been left with an uncle for the duration. When the dust had settled and the lawyers had departed, Allen was left with a hundred and thirty million in assets and stock options and a battle on his hands from his father's former partner on who owned what. As a result of the prolonged and ugly nature of the case he was left at the mercy of a man who cared nothing for him. He ran off at fifteen, opting to live on the streets rather than continue subjecting himself to his uncle's abusive behavior. He would have been dead inside a week if he hadn't encountered Frances on his second day.

He was hunched over behind a dumpster, having been robbed of all his belongings but not yet hungry enough to sift through the garbage for food. Frances was just coming off her shift; she worked as a collector for a local bookie and had just finished her rounds. Sure she was a small girl but she was also fast and she knew how to use a baseball bat to lethal effect. She didn't have to mostly; the customers she collected from knew her, knew who she represented; and knew what would happen to them if they tried anything weird. It was illegal sure, and she spent approximately half her time dodging the cops but it beat turning tricks for a living. Normally, she didn't try to get too involved with other street kids; they tended to want to suck you into their sorry existences – whether it was sex or drugs or both. It was a downhill destination and Frances wasn't having any of it. She had a plan, and she was getting out, going straight and legit. She was going to be a writer. She already wrote; had pages and pages of short stories beneath her bed. She wanted to get a locker to store it all in; she knew that the bunker where she stayed wasn't safe from vandals. Still it was as secure as she could make it and it would have to do for now. Something about this kid made her stop though. He wasn't the usual type of street kid. She couldn't quite put her finger on why though. Maybe it was that his face was just too clean; or his hands were free of tracks…anyway, whatever the reason; she stopped and stared at him.

"Whassup witchu?" she asked him. He looked right miserable slumped as he was between the dumpster and the brick wall that housed the neighborhood soup kitchen. It wouldn't be open for at least another four hours. He looked up at her with the most extraordinary gray eyes she'd ever seen.

"Leave me alone," he said dully, sounding defeated by life already.

Frances hesitated; she really should do as he said and keep walking. Her bed was calling.

"You need help man?" she asked instead.

He stared at her speculatively and she wondered what he was seeing.

*****

What Allen was seeing was a petite dark haired light skinned black girl with green eyes and the most unkempt hair he'd ever seen on a female. It was long almost reaching halfway down her diminutive frame and looked like it had about zero acquaintance with a comb. She looked like a strong breeze could blow her over in spite of the baseball bat she was holding in her tiny hand. She couldn't be more than ten years old and here she was asking *him* if she could help him?

"I got a bunker if you need somewhere to sleep," she said, he couldn't tell if her complexion was naturally glowy or she was blushing. Surely she wasn't suggesting…

"You really shouldn't invite strange men to follow you home you know," he told her chidingly.

She laughed. He raised his eyebrows in disbelief as she stood there laughing at him, a deep rich honeyed belly laugh that seemed to come right from the center of her being. He frowned at her, wondering what was so funny.

"Are you coming or not?" she asked still smiling.

Allen was tired of the cold hard ground. He would be glad of a softer surface to lie down on, maybe somewhere warmer. Maybe she had some food she'd be happy to share with him?

He didn't like to take advantage of a kid, but he was cold, hungry and tired.

"Sure, I'll come," he said standing up.

He followed her through convoluted alleyways until she disappeared into a doorway he wouldn't have seen if he wasn't specifically looking for it. He followed her tentatively, wondering for the first time if this was a trick of some sort. The inside of the building was dark and dank; with the far off whiff of sewage permeating the air.

"Stay close," her voice floated back to him from some point ahead. He hastened his footsteps to keep her white reflector jacket in sight. It was the only thing he could see in the black hallway. He heard a door open and then she switched on a light and he could see into the room. It was tiny, with a mattress on the floor, another baseball bat, a cardboard box with items on it that might be knick knacks or treasured family heirlooms for all Allen knew. There were also two pairs of shoes resting neatly side by side next to the bed; a pair of

Nike sneakers and a pair of black boots. Allen's eyes traveled to her feet; she was wearing another pair of sneakers, threadbare and old.

"You can have the floor," she said gesturing to an empty corner of the small room. He crossed to it as she flopped onto the mattress, fiddling with something Allen couldn't see. The whir of a machine suddenly filled the room with sound and Frances placed a small box like gadget next to her mattress. The room warmed slowly.

"Electric heater," she said burrowing into her duvet and curling up. "Goodnight."

Frances seemed to drop off to sleep and Allen was surprised at her ability to just relax her guard in front of a total stranger like him. Surely she knew better than that! Sure she had her baseball bat next to her but still…he looked around searching for something to use as a pillow. There was a pile of clothes nearby and he pulled the whole thing closer and placed his head on it. It was soft and the room was warm. He folded his hands on his chest and went to sleep.

*****

He woke to the smell of food permeating the tiny space. His stomach growled in response to the stimuli and he sat up almost before he'd even thought about it. Frances was fiddling with two paper plates containing French fries and cheeseburgers.

“Good morning,” she said without looking up.

“Morning,”, he replied eyes on the food.

“Bathroom is down the hall if you want to freshen up,” she said. Allen struggled to his feet.

“Thank you,” he said padding across the room and opening the door. The hall wasn't so dark, a sliver of light illuminated the way to the bathroom. Allen hoped it wasn't too gross; he put his shoes back on and walked cautiously down the hall. He pushed open the door, instinctively holding his breath. The bathroom though, was surprisingly clean. Clearly someone took the trouble to keep it that way. Allen used the facilities and then washed his face and hands and went back to the room.

"What is this place?" he asked. "Do you live here by yourself?"

Frances just looked at him with an inscrutable glance. "You didn't give your name," she said.

"Allen. Allen St. James. And you are…?"

"Frances Hilton," she said.

"Oh. Any relation…?" he asked half joking.

"Sure. I'm related to the hotel mogul; it's why I'm living in this palace."

"No need for sarcasm," he mumbled sitting down next to her and taking the plate she handed him. He tucked into the food concentrating on eating. He needed to find a way to pay her back for the food and board. Maybe he could offer to be her bodyguard?

"How can I repay your kindness?" he asked.

Frances said nothing just continued to eat; only darting an eloquent glance in his direction as if to tell him to shut up. He continued to eat in silence, taking her lead.

*****

“So why did you run away from home?” she asked after they’d eaten. Allen jumped; somehow, he hadn’t expected that question.

“How did you know?” he asked.

“You’re no street kid,” she said, her eyes on the shoes she was lacing.

“Wow, is it that obvious?” he asked wryly.

“Kind of is, yeah,” she replied straightening up and looking at him. Allen shrugged.

“Okay then, yeah I ran. I don’t feel like talking about it though, if you don’t mind.”

“I don’t mind. You mind pullin your weight?” she asked.

Allen was cautious about agreeing to things blind but she’d proved legit so far. “Sure, I’d like to. Just tell me how.”

“Come with me,” she said heading for the door.

*****

Karl Valence, her employer and local bookie was only too happy to take on another collector. Business was good and kids were cheap. Besides, Allen looked like a capable individual if a bit soft. At fifteen years old, he was already six feet tall and well built. Karl decided to pair him with Frances; she was a tough cookie but small. If she had ‘enforcement’ with her he could expand her scope of collection. She was a remarkably effective collector; never left without getting her cash. Karl had his eye on her.

Allen and Frances worked well together; they complemented each other quite well and Karl was happy with the work they did. Allen had been reported missing by his uncle though, because you couldn’t be the guardian for someone if they weren’t present and accounted for and his uncle had been cut off until Allen was found. A reward had been put out for his recovery; and one of the clients they collected from recognized Allen. He wasn't about to pass up a two hundred thousand dollar pay day so he called the number given on the poster. Two days later, police showed up at their bunker and tried to take Allen away. He refused to leave Frances behind despite her reassurances that she would be just fine. Allen's uncle was not on board with having another mouth to feed but Allen went around him and spoke to the administrators himself. His three months on the street had taught him to stand up for himself and he felt like Frances was the only real friend he'd ever had. At least the only friend who wanted nothing from him. All she had done was look after him and helped him without asking for anything in return. Allen owed her.

The administrators proposed a one off pay off to Frances but Allen felt that would be too tacky. Besides he was pretty sure Frances would refuse it. His counter proposal was that they could take her in. The administrators were reluctant to do that and insisted on doing a background check on her. Allen was fine with that, if only because she'd kept her history pretty close to her chest and Allen was curious. It was a typical story though; her mother was a crack addict who over dosed one day when Frances was ten years old. Frances was home at the time and waited for two days for her mother to come home. When she didn't, and Frances got hungry, she ventured out to look for her and for food. For a few days, she surfed the dumpsters, and filched fruit at the market. She avoided soup kitchens because they might want to know where her guardian or parent was. Even at ten years old, she knew what could happen to her and she wanted no part of foster homes and she didn't want to leave her mother. She went back to the apartment to sleep and check to see if her mother had returned; until the landlord threw her out for not paying rent. Then she was out on the street, alone and penniless. She was a survivor though and quickly found an abandoned building to live in. She joined up with Karl Valence not long after. The administrators were worried that Frances would bring her shady past into Allen's life with her and tried to dissuade him from his plan to give her shelter. Frances was fine with just going back to her crib; she had lived on the street for four years; she was used to it.

"Shut up and eat your breakfast," Allen said the first time Frances tried to suggest she mosey on out and head back to the bunker before someone else discovered it.

"Why? Would you want to do this to yourself. You don't really know me-" she began to say.

"You didn't know me when you took me home with you," he interrupted her.

"Yeah well..." Frances smiled and shrugged one shoulder.

"You wouldn't have survived a week on your own."

"True," Allen agreed smiling back.

"You don't owe me anything," Frances said.

"Sure I don't. Do you not want to stay with me?" he asked.

“What’s not to want?”Frances asked spreading out her hands to indicate the lavishness of the room they were breakfasting in.

“Well then? Stay.”

“Okay then.”

“Cool,” Allen said happily.

“What shall I do while you’re in school all day?” she asked.

Allen frowned at her. “You’ll come with me,” he said, like it was a foregone conclusion.

Frances frowned. “I don’t think so. I don’t really have any formal education; I’d have to go to the first grade or something.”

Allen looked perturbed. “Oh…well. We could hire a tutor,” he suggested.

“Hey, don’t stir yourself on my account, I’ll be fine.”

Allen said nothing but the next week, he went to discuss with his administrators the possibility of getting a tutor for Frances. They told him that as guardian, his uncle would have to sign off on that. Allen knew his uncle was resentful of Frances' presence in their household, he called her a gold digger to her face and was rude to her when Allen wasn't around. Still, Allen had learned to stand up to him, stand his ground; so he knew he would get what he wanted. He had his uncle's number now, knew how to handle him. So he went in with a proposal; he would agree to endow his uncle with ten million dollars as soon as he attained his majority if he didn't stand in the way of Frances staying with them, and signing off on anything they needed him to. If he refused, Allen would leave him on the street as soon as he was legal. His uncle could hardly refuse. Frances got a tutor and Allen's uncle signed off on her staying with them. She wasn't in the system which meant nobody was looking for her. She would have to get into the system at some point, if she wanted to be a productive member of society so Allen had his lawyers working on that.

Frances turned out to be pretty bright and soaked up knowledge like a sponge. Her tutor was very impressed with her progress and informed Allen's uncle as the legal guardian that he most likely had a genius on his hands. Since Michael St. James couldn't care less how bright Frances was, he just grunted and handed the tutor his check for the week.

*****

Allen was a popular boy in high school. He had street cred for running away from home...And bringing back a street kid to live with him. He was also an orphan, a rich one at that, which added to his allure. He had no problem getting dates but he didn't really have a steady girlfriend. He didn't feel like anyone really understood him...except maybe Frances. She was his best friend and confidante. She made no effort to fit in with his school friends, tending to go off on her own with a book. But she always had time for him. His friends thought she was a strange girl, whose hair could use a trim maybe, possibly a stylist. Frances thought it was a huge compromise that she combed it everyday so she wasn't about to sit in a salon chair and allow herself to be transformed into some stranger just so

Allen's friends could feel that she was less strange. She was strange, she accepted that; she didn't see how it was anybody's problem but hers. she figured she was making a major concession combing her hair every day.

When Allen was eighteen he met a girl; she was new in town, worked at the coffee shop where he stopped off every morning on the way to school. She was tall and blonde; beautiful in a fragile sort of way. Even though she was almost five foot eleven, there was something delicate about her that awakened Allen's protective instincts. The first time they met, her boyfriend was bothering her at work, and her supervisor was inclined to let her go because of it; he had no time for that sort of drama in his establishment. Allen stepped in, defended her and saved her job. He also gave her (ex) boyfriend a black eye. It was the beginning of a tumultuous relationship.

Frances didn't like her on sight; she felt that Kristen was too clingy, needy and manipulative for Allen's good. She didn't try to step between them though – she knew it was none of her business much as she wanted to tell him to kick her to the curb. She kept to herself instead, especially when Kristen was around. Kristen didn't like her either; she viewed her as too much of a threat since she lived in Allen's house and was his best friend. She tried her best to drive a wedge between them as subtly as she could. She came over during the weekends to see him, and when she found them together, she got sulky. She tried to complain to Allen about Frances 'always' being around like she was cock blocking them. Allen didn't see it though; he was used to Frances always curled up somewhere nearby with a book. It comforted him to know she was there. And she didn't really stop them from doing anything. They could make out if they wanted, or even get to third base, Frances didn't so much as look up. She'd seen her fill of sexual acts on the street; she had told him that she had no interest in voyeurism as a result. Allen wondered sometimes if she'd maybe experienced more than witnessing sexual acts because she seemed to have absolutely no interest. It worried him sometimes, how aloof she was from the whole teenage romance scene but then she didn't go to school; maybe she just hadn't met anyone she was interested in. Still, Allen preferred not to leave her completely to her own devices and he didn't see why Kristen couldn't just get along with her. Matters came to a head when Kristen reached a point where she felt comfortable enough to issue an ultimatum. Frances or her. She accused Allen of wanting his cake and eating it too; implying that the reason he wanted Frances around was because he was sleeping with her. He assured her that wasn't the case and that was when she said, "Choose between us." She was very surprised when Allen chose Frances. She was even more surprised that it was not an agonizing decision; as soon as the ultimatum was issued, Allen and Kristen were done.

Chapter 2

“Kristen and I are done,” Allen said the next day at breakfast.

“Aww, why?” Frances fake whined as she stuffed sausage and mushrooms into her mouth.

“She was getting a little too big for her boots. She actually told me to get rid of you.”

“I’m touched. I didn’t know you cared.”

“Well I do. Plus I need to prepare for finals, I don’t have time for shenanigans,” he said.

Frances laughed, “That’s the Allen I know and love; practical to the end of time.”

“Mostly it was her asking me to choose between her and you though,” he qualified smiling as he forked his eggs into his mouth.

“I think she was just threatened. You’re living with a girl who isn’t related to you; there’s no girlfriend who would like that.”

“Are you defending her?”

“No. I’m just seeing the other side. I get it. I wouldn’t want some hot black girl living with my boyfriend either.”

Allen laughed, “Hot black girl…Jesus Frances, you have jokes.”

“That’s not nice,” Frances protested.

“But it's true,” he said. Frances flashed him the finger but kept eating. Allen stared speculatively at her.

“So…about college…” he said.

“Yeah?” Frances replied spinning her bacon onto a fork.

“Are you going to apply?”

Frances laughed from her belly. “What? Me?” she asked incredulously. “I just learned how to read.”

Allen was silent for a while, pondering the best way to tell her she had everything it took to succeed as a college student or life in general.

“What?” Frances demanded.

“You put yourself down a little too much for my taste,” Allen replied.

“Well, I’m sorry I’m such a disappointment to you,” Frances said, she actually sounded hurt.

Allen sighed. “You’re not a disappointment, don’t be an idiot. You just put yourself down so much. See? Like now,” he said anticipating her snarky reply.

Frances made a face at him, “Well there’s one way to sort this shit out; I’ll apply and then you can read through all the rejection letters and burn them.”

“Deal,” Allen replied.

Frances stared at him, as if waiting for the punch line. Allen continued to eat his breakfast unperturbed, however so, she went back to her own and decided to ignore him.

*****

They both got into the University of Minnesota; it was the only campus they both applied to that they both got into. Frances was in shock that she got more than one acceptance letter so she was quite willing to let Allen guide her as to which to choose. He was legal now and able to take charge of his parents' fortune. He paid his uncle the money he promised and then sold the house. He didn't want any reminders of his childhood; the death of his parents weighed heavily on that house, and the abuse his uncle had subjected him to. The only good memories the house had was after Frances came to live with them. He was ready to let it go. Let the whole town go in fact and start fresh. His administrators were opposed to such drastic changes and did their best to dissuade him. He only convinced them by pointing out the financial impracticality of maintaining a house in Prosperity, Indiana when he was going to spend the majority of the next four years in St. Paul Minnesota. It made more economic sense simply to get an apartment in Falcon Heights; after all it wasn't like he had relatives to come back to in Prosperity. The administrators agreed that this was a plan and Allen and Frances packed up the house.

Frances was very insecure about her suitability to be a college student but Allen rode roughshod all over her objections and signed her up for whatever classes he thought might interest her. This included linguistics, French, literature and history. At that point, Frances took over and chose her own classes. Freshman year of college was a period of adjustment; the freedom was intoxicating for Allen; but Frances had always been unencumbered by adult supervision so it was par for the course for her. Allen tried everything on offer from LSD to sky diving. He spent the minimum time he could actually in class that would enable him to pass his exams. Frances on the other hand, spent all her time in class, or at the library catching up on the quieter side of growing up. They still lived together at an apartment off campus but somehow, they rarely saw each other.

Frances met a guy in the library in the beginning of sophomore year. He was intense in a way that fascinated her; his ambitions were boundless and he came from a poor background too. He was only able to study at the U of M because of a scholarship and financial aid. He wanted to get his degree and go home to change his neighborhood. Frances fell in love with his passion and he fell in love with her brain and her sass. Allen was against it. He did everything he could to dissuade Frances from going out with him.

"Look at him with those dreadlocks. Its so pretentious; who does he think he is? Bob Marley?" Allen said sneering derisively at Kareem who was checking out some books as Frances and Allen waited.

"Don't be jealous," Frances said amused. "I still love you."

Allen slapped at her arm with the back of his hand, "I'm being serious."

"So am I!" she protested.

"What is it anyway? You lookin' to get laid or something? Because I'm pretty sure I know a few guys who are more experienced than that Sean Paul wannabe you hangin' with."

Frances laughed. "Have you been taking surveys?" she asked amused. "Or are you relying on locker room boasts; because you might not know this man, but boys lie. All the time."

Allen glared at her, “I know that chica; I’m trying to help you here.”

Frances turned to face him, “Allen, I like him okay? Do I try to get between you and *your* girlfriends?”

“Ha! What about Kristen?”

“What about her? I didn’t tell you to get rid of her; you did that all by your damn self.”

“Yeah but it was coz of you,” Allen said.

“Fine. But Kareem’s not asking me to choose between you and him so you can just step off Allen. Green is not a good look on you.”

Allen snorted, “As if. I’m not jealous.”

“Whatever you say slugger,” Frances said smiling as Kareem came up to them.

“Got the books,” he said. “Can’t wait to debate the merits and demerits of Homer with you.”

He was grinning at Frances which annoyed Allen to no end. He pulled her away from Kareem as they were walking to the car.

“You know I can debate Homer just as good as he can,” he hissed at her.

She just laughed and pulled her hand out of his grip, hurrying forward to walk with Kareem. Allen had a date that night but he blew it off to lounge in the study watching Frances and Kareem read and talk about The Odyssey. He was pretending to study as he did it but Frances wasn’t fooled. He was seriously cock blocking her.

“You want to like, take this to my room?” she asked Kareem. Allen took a very deep breath and seemed like he was about to stand up and maybe block the door.

“Sure I do,” Kareem replied face brightening visibly. He glanced at Allen as if aware of his cock blocking intentions and then stood up, holding out his hand to help Frances up. Allen stood too, wanting to stall with something but not thinking of something in time. Frances and Kareem strode past him, headed toward her room. Allen followed them with his narrowed eyes. He was surprised at how much he wanted to ram the switch blade he always carried on his person into Kareem's heart. He hadn't experienced such violent thoughts since a random druggie had almost knifed Frances for the money she was carrying when they were still living on the street. Allen wondered at it; maybe he'd developed a paternal complex and was treating Frances as if she was his daughter? Somehow, Allen didn't think so…

He waited twenty minutes and then strode over to Frances' door, knocking loudly. There was silence from inside which was making Allen feel like breaking down the door to see what they were up to. He was just assessing it for sturdiness when it opened suddenly.

"What?" Frances asked irritably.

"I need to talk to you," he said to her.

She lifted up her eyebrow in inquiry.

“In private,” he said.

Frances sighed, looked into the room with an, “Excuse me”, and then stepped out and shut the door behind her.

“What’s going on Allen?” she asked.

He leaned down and put his lips on hers. She stiffened in surprise and he was just as surprised as she was. It hadn’t been his intention to do that. He hadn’t known what his intentions were but they weren’t that. Still, now that his lips were on hers, he found himself wanting to explore the inside of her mouth, taste her, know the texture and softness of her lips. He was surprised how soft her lips were; she was such a hard ass on the outside, he expected them to be more chapped, not so plush and soft; tempting a body to lean in and squash them against his own lips; suck them open and insert his tongue inside her mouth. And she was letting him; he wondered if she was still in shock or if she wanted to kiss him back.

He lifted his head and looked into her green eyes flecked with gold. They were wide and staring at him as if she'd never seen him before. He cleared his throat and straightened up.

"Umm," he said.

"What was that?" she whispered hoarsely.

Allen shrugged and continued to stare into her eyes. He shouldn't be thinking it, but all he wanted to do was kiss her again.

"Please tell me you didn't just kiss me so I'd get rid of Kareem," she hissed.

"What? No! It…it just happened," he protested.

She bit her lower lip making Allen jealous of her teeth; *he* wanted to bite her lower lip. She was looking at him pretty skeptically and he should probably be paying attention to that.

"I'm not sorry though," he said.

She lifted her eyebrows. "You're not sorry for what?" she asked eyes still wide and staring.

"I'm not sorry I kissed you. Are you sorry I kissed you?"

"Oh God, I'm not having this conversation. Go to sleep Allen," Frances said walking back to her room and slamming the door behind her. Allen stood in the hallway and just watched her door for a bit. After an interminable amount of time, he decided to just go and sleep. There was nothing more he could do right now. He opened the door to his room and flopped on his bed, watching the hallway hopefully. Surely she was going to get him to leave…she wouldn't do this to him, would she?

Allen sat up until 2am waiting and *finally* the door to Frances' room opened. Kareem padded down the hall, in nothing but his boxers and a wife beater. He did a double take as he passed Allen's door and saw him sitting on the bed staring into the hallway.

"Whoa man, you scared me," he said with a laugh. Allen just glared at him. Kareem saw that he wasn't getting anywhere with him and went on his way, using *Allen's* house; drinking his water, peeing in his toilet and sleeping on the bed *he* bought. Allen was ready to commit bloody murder. In the morning, he started awake and realized he'd fallen asleep sitting on the end of his bed. He got up, ignoring his complaining muscles and walked to his doorway, peering down the hall at Frances' door. It was wide open, and the bed was made. It was also empty. Allen looked the other way, towards the kitchen, but there wasn't anybody there either. The apartment was silent.

He went to the grocery store to restock the fridge and then decided to attend his afternoon classes. When he got home at six pm, it was to find Frances seated cross legged on his bed, looking like butter wouldn't melt in her mouth.

"Well hello there," he said coming into his room and shutting the door behind him. She stared back at him impassively.

"What? You won't talk to me?" he asked coming to sit at the edge of his own bed.

“What was that yesterday Allen? What were you trying to do?” she demanded eyes narrowed, practically shooting sparks at him.

“I was trying…to show you how I feel,” he said looking down at his blue carpet.

“Really? Coz it felt like you were trying to manipulate me into doing what you wanted,” she accused. Allen looked up into her eyes, hurt in his own.

“How can you think that after everything we’ve been through together?” he asked.

“How could you do that after everything we’ve been through together?” she countered.

Allen’s face reddened though he hesitated to call it blushing.

“What did I do that was so bad? I was just showing you how I feel.”

“Oh? You just discovered these feelings the minute I got a boyfriend?” she asked snarkily.

“Boyfriend? Really? Him?” Allen said completely distracted.

“Yes. Boyfriend. Kareem is my boyfriend and you will deal.”

Allen stared at her uncomprehendingly. “You can’t be serious,” he said at last.

“Why not?” Frances challenged.

“You kissed me back yesterday. I felt it,” he said.

“You took me by surprise,” Frances said.

“But..” Allen began.

“No buts Allen, this is how it is. You need to accept it.”

Allen said nothing further, just stood up and walked out. He also accepted nothing – he resolved to make it his life’s work to get rid of Kareem if it was the last thing he did.

*****

In spite of his best efforts, Kareem and Frances lasted a whole year. It was the most miserable year of Allen’s life and he made sure Frances knew it. She responded by spending less and less time with him; they were drifting away from each other slowly but surely. It made Frances really sad but there was only so much she could do without giving in to Allen’s manipulations. At the end of the year though, Kareem came out to her; he told her that he loved her, so he couldn't continue to lie to her. He was a transgender individual and he felt like it was time he embraced it and accepted it about himself. He hoped that Frances could accept it too.

She could; but only as a friend. If Kareem's ultimate goal was to be a female, that was fine, but Frances wasn't a lesbian. She wanted a man who wanted to *be* a man. Their break up was amicable but Frances didn't tell Allen about it. There was just too much poison in that well.

"How come Kareem doesn't stay over anymore, and you guys aren't joined at the hip?"

"How is that any of your business?"

"Hey, I'm just a concerned friend. If you don't want to tell me, fine," Allen said throwing his hands in the air.

Frances hesitated, watching him for a moment. "We broke up," she said at last.

“What? Seriously? When? Why didn’t you tell me?” Allen asked all up in her face, the his face became thunderous. “What did he do?”

Frances pushed him away, “Allen relax, it was mutual; we want different things, we’re still friends though.”

Allen glared at her. “What do I look like? Oprah? This isn’t a talk show and you don’t get to speak in clichés with me.”

Frances sighed and closed her eyes and then opened them. “It's not my news to tell Allen. Just know that he didn’t do anything, I didn’t do anything. It was just…the situation.”

Allen leaned back on the chair staring at her. “So he’s gay huh?”

Frances rolled her eyes but didn’t reply.

Allen jumped up in glee. “I knew it! I knew there was something...” he began.

“He’s not *gay*!” Frances yelled. “Now could you please leave it alone?”

“Fine,” Allen said sitting back down and studying her closely. “You don’t look heart broken.”

Frances looked up at him, narrowing her eyes in annoyance. “What? Not enough gorging on ice cream and lounging about in my pajamas for you?”

Allen shrugged. “Well its kind of hard to comfort someone if they don’t look miserable,” he said making Frances laugh.

“You could always buy me a jeep to cheer me up; it's way more fun than whatever ‘comforting’ you had in mind.”

“You’re all heart Frances,” he said wryly.

“Aren’t I just? Now finish your breakfast and go to class,” she ordered standing up and lifting her heavy duty bag. She actually had a Honda that she’d insisted on buying herself from her savings. Over the years, she’d done various odd jobs, including presently working in the campus library. It was an old car, but reliable and it was all hers. Allen had offered to upgrade her many times but she’d always refused so she assumed he knew she was joking about the jeep.

When she got home that evening there was a brand new dark green jeep sitting in the driveway with a massive bow on the front. A small crowd of their neighbors was standing around, admiring it and a slight cheer went up when they saw her. Frances stopped and stared at the car, hoping it was someone else's who was maybe currently behind her and that was why everyone was staring in her direction. She walked slowly toward the group, looking for Allen but he wasn't there.

"Hey Frances, Allen left this here for you. He asked us to watch out for it and give you this when you arrived," Carlton, who lived a floor below them said holding out a key to her.

She stared at it and then at the car and then back to the keys, and then up to Carlton's face. He was grinning like a loon.

"Where is he?" she asked.

Carlton shrugged. "Dunno. He left," he said not very helpfully.

He was still holding out the keys so Frances took them with a fake smile and turned to the car.

"You gonna take it for a test drive?" Carlton asked excitedly.

“Nah, I think I’ll just…drive it into the garage for now,” she said to everyone’s disappointment. The apartment complex had a two car garage for every apartment. Frances parked the jeep in Allen’s spot and then drove her Honda into her spot. Allen could park his car in the driveway for all she cared. The crowd had thankfully dispersed by the time she emerged from the garage and she went up to their apartment and shut the door behind her, planning her words carefully. She made to step further into the apartment when she froze, noticing the petals on the floor for the first time. It was a carpet of red petals, leading to…she walked forward to see. They meandered down the hall to the dining area where the room was dimmed with closed blinds. The table was laid for two and soft music was playing from the speakers. There was a man in the kitchen, fiddling about with something on the cooker.

“Hello?” she called uncertainly, wondering if she should be calling the police right now. He turned around and smiled at her.

“Ah, Ms. Hilton; welcome. I am to inform you that dinner will be served promptly at seven. There is a dress on your bed and you have thirty minutes if you wish to freshen up,” he said with a smile before turning back to his delicious smelling concoctions. Frances hesitated, wanting to ask more questions but she didn’t want to put this strange man in a spot. Clearly, he was here with permission. She padded to her room, where the rose petals were arranged in a heart around her bed, in the midst of which lay a dress. Lying atop the dress was a note, and Frances sighed in relief.

“At last, an explanation,” she said aloud hurrying forward to pick it up.

Hey Frannie,

How you doing? The dress is vintage Chanel, the shoes are Louboutins. Please oblige me by not making a fuss; just put the damned clothes on, comb your hair for once and let’s have a nice dinner. Whatever happens after that is up to you. Okay?

www.SaucyRomanceBooks.com/RomanceBooks

Love,

Your best friend, Allen.

Chapter 3

Frances was torn between stubborn recalcitrance and curiosity. She wanted to see where this was going but she didn't want to do as she was told. It would set a dangerous precedent if this was what she thought it was. Still, she stepped in the shower and washed everything including her hair. She blow dried it without a comb so it fell in random curls all the way down her back and then ran her fingers through it to simulate a comb. She picked up the white dress; it was short and fit her like a glove. Her boobs were half exposed in the deep V of the neckline but there was a string of pearls sitting beside the dress that she could use to partially cover those up. The dress ended just above her knees and combined with the six inch Louboutins, they gave the illusion that she was much taller than her five foot five. There were also pearl earrings in the stash and a bracelet as well. She walked a bit unsteadily out of the room and down the hall to the dining area. Allen was there, standing waiting for her in a black tux. He had a bunch of red roses in his hand and as she wobbled toward him, he stretched out a hand to help her out.

“Careful now,” he murmured as he led her to their table and laid the flowers next to her.

“Is this a date?” she asked right off.

“Ding ding ding! Give the lady a gold bracelet,” he replied, reaching into his pocket and extracting an actual gold bracelet which he slipped onto the wrist not sporting the pearl bracelet.

“Allen,” she began to protest.

“Shut up,” he replied reaching for his napkin. She stared at him, eyebrows raised but he ignored her and continued arranging his napkin to his satisfaction. He looked over at her to see if she was doing the same and found her still watching him. He sighed and leaned back looking back at her.

“Okay fine, it’s a date. We’re on a date. I’m decking you with expensive presents which I know you don’t like but I’ve wanted to do this forever and now we're taking our relationship to the next level, I'm allowed," he said.

She narrowed her eyes at him. "We're taking our relationship to the next level? Wow, someone forgot to drop me a memo."

Allen was silent, staring at his plate for a bit. "Do you not... want me?"

"So not the point Allen," she replied right away.

"Well then, what *is* the point?" he asked.

"The point is, you can't go making arbitrary life changes for me as if I was your pet or a piece of furniture!" she said or rather yelled.

"I don't think you're a piece of furniture!" he protested or rather yelled back.

"Well, you're sure treating me like one," she countered.

"You're the most important thing in my life. I don't know what I would do without you. I thought you felt the same about me," Allen said.

"And this is how you show it?"

"With wine and dinner and presents? When did that become a bad thing? There are so many girls who would *die* to be in your place!"

Frances stood up abruptly, wobbling a bit in her six inch heels. "Well then go get one of them and enjoy your dinner," she shouted before stomping off to her room, kicking off her shoes before she'd walked three steps. She slammed her door, struggling out of the dress as soon as she'd gotten it closed. She flopped down on the bed, in a ring of roses, in her underwear and stared at the ceiling. Her eyes were stinging and there was a lump in her throat but she ignored them in favor of studying the patterns on the ceiling. She wondered if it was time for her to move out. Their situation was so complicated; for one thing, Allen was paying for her college tuition, she was living in his house, eating his food…she guessed it was just one step to sleeping in his bed. But she hadn't lived the life she had only to end up being *that* girl.

There was a tentative knock on the door.

“Frances? Please can I come in?” Allen asked from the other side. He sounded close to tears too. Frances said nothing but she heard the knob turn and he was opening the door. She just watched him as he poked his head in slowly, like a turtle emerging from its shell. She wanted to laugh but the lump was still in her throat and she was afraid of what would happen if she opened her mouth. He stretched his hand into the room and hanging from his fingers was a white handkerchief which he waved up and down. Frances couldn’t help the soundless laugh that escaped her. when he saw it, his face lightened and he stepped fully into her room.

“I am crap at seducing women. Too used to them falling at my feet.”

He looked at her, waiting for some sort of response but she just continued to lay curled on her bed, looking like temptation personified.

“Please tell me what to do or say to make this okay,” he said.

Her eyes swiveled to look at him, judging his sincerity and then she shrugged and sat up.

“How about you tell me where all this is coming from Allen. One minute, we’re barely talking, the next, you’re tossing presents at me like I’m a stripper in a club: what gives?”

Allen took a deep breath, and a step closer to her. “I guess you haven’t noticed since you’ve been so wrapped up in Kareem this past year, but I’ve been waiting for you,” he said gray eyes trained on green with painful honesty. “I realized when I started fantasizing about putting a knife in Kareem’s throat the first night he stayed over here, that my feelings for you were far from platonic. I tried to tell you but…”

Frances sat up, forgetting that she was wearing nothing but underwear, intent on Allen’s words. He dropped his eyes to his own feet so he could continue.

“Anyway, so this year has literally been hell for me. Like… literally. I never want to go through something like it again. So when you told me that you and Kareem were *finally* broken up

I decided that I wouldn't wait even one more day. Maybe give you a chance to hook up with someone else…I can still taste you on my lips you know? That time you kissed me back? I just wanted…" he trailed off, voice cutting off with too much emotion.

Frances got up, stepping over her heart of roses and came to stand facing him, studying his face intently. To his credit, he kept his eyes on hers, not even straying an inch downwards to her boobs encased only in a bra.

"So why couldn't you just say so?" she asked.

Allen's breath hitched as he stared at her, hope blooming in his eyes. He studied her face, looking for, she knew not what and then he lurched forward grabbing at her shoulders as his lips came down on hers. He squashed his lips into hers as his fingers dug painfully into her arms. Her own hands came up dislodging his from her shoulders as she hooked them around his neck. His hands dropped to her waist and he wrapped his hands around her bringing her tight against him as he continued to plunder her mouth with his. He lifted her up and walked with her to the bed, laying her on it without so much as moving his lips from hers. His tongue continued its exploration of her mouth even as his hands unhooked her bra and tossed it, and then her panties. She lay beneath him, naked and exposed as his hands touched her everywhere igniting a fire everywhere they landed and causing her to moan with need into his mouth, trying to get him closer. He was still fully dressed in his tuxedo and she detached her lips from his, much to his protests, and pushed him away. His face fell as he thought she was rejecting him.

"Take off your clothes," she ordered and he brightened, hastening to comply. He stood up tossing his clothes every which way; jacket and shirt, bow tie and pants and then his under clothes. He was back on the bed with a flump, taking Frances' breath away with his immediacy and enthusiasm.

"I love you; you know that right?" he said before plundering her lips again and preventing her reply. She wrapped her arms and legs around him and pulled him close to show him that, yes; she knew. He bit her bottom lip like he'd wanted to do all those months ago and then licked a trail down her jaw to her neck and collar bone as his hands took hold of her thighs and pulled them further apart.

"Want you so much," he said into the skin of her chest just above her breasts before taking one nipple into his mouth and sucking. Frances jerked with the sensation it caused to go shooting down her body and causing her to leak wetness into the sheets.

"Allen," she breathed as her own hands found his nipples, and began to squeeze and fondle them. He made a pained sound of arousal snapping his hips and gripping her thighs so hard there were sure to be bruises there the next day. She rubbed his nipples harder, nipping at his powerful shoulder as she did so and he cried out, hips arching of their own volition. She could feel his hardness against her like a steel band and then his thumb trailed forward, breaching her center and exploring inside, seeking the sensitive nub that needed no further stimulation really. He rubbed back and forth against it and her back arched in response, mouth open, head thrown back.

“I need you Allen,” she cried. “Now!”

It was an order he wasn’t ready to refuse.

“Condom?” he asked desperately, his face red, veins bulging. He didn’t want to leave her to go find his wallet or his bedside table to get one so he was really hoping she kept some close by. The thought of her using condoms with anyone but him though got him hot in a whole other way and he growled deep in his throat. She reached out and opened her bedside table, handing him one. He snatched it out of her hand, tearing savagely at the packaging as she watched in puzzlement and then slipped it on. His hands on her thighs were a bit rougher than they’d been before as he spread them and thrust into her. She made a sound in her throat, half pleasure, half pain and the red haze of jealousy cleared a little for him to see *her*. His touch gentled and he leaned in to kiss her softly in wordless apology. His movements slowed and deepened as he used every thrust to hit a sensitive spot inside of her. She spread her hands out in surrender, eyes closed as she made noises of satisfaction and surrender. Her legs wrapped tight around his waist, she lifted her pelvis to meet thrust for thrust, wanting him as deep inside her as he wanted to go.

“Frannie Fran Fran my Frances,” he murmured incoherently in her ear as he pushed into her hips, stuttering with need. She pulled at his hair to turn his head so she could fit her lips to his, kissing into his mouth with the same rhythm he was thrusting into her. He groaned with desire.

“Who taught you how to do that?” he asked pulling away from her and thrusting into her harder at the same time. She pulled his mouth back to hers without answering and he lost himself in the taste of her, her intoxicating odor surrounding him with want and need and the feeling of being home. Her arms tightened around his neck and her legs around his hips as her back arched and she shuddered, releasing wetness and warmth around him. The thought that he had made her come caused him to spasm with savage release as his vision whitened and he let himself go.

“Oh baby,” he said as he slumped against her neck, burrowing his nose deep into her shoulder so he was surrounded by the smell of satiated sex, the sandalwood scent that she used and her own unique musk. He could lie there forever just breathing her in. She turned her head to lay a sweet kiss on his shoulder and he reared back to withdraw from her so he could take off the condom. He wanted to stay inside her forever and as he threw the condom in the bedside basket his half hard dick was already seeking her warmth.

“Let me just lay in you for a minute okay?” he murmured as he pushed into her. She let him do it, opening for him as he plunged as deep as his rapidly hardening cock could go. He bit her neck and then kissed it, laving her skin with his tongue and sucking and biting.

“Oooh, that feels good,” she sighed, tilting her head to give him more room to molest her.

“Yeah, well get used to it,” he said, pressing into her as he sucked her neck harder. He got up on his elbows eventually and looked down at her, smiling into her eyes.

“This feels right doesn’t it?” he asked as his hips gyrated in slow circles, driving her mad.

“Yeah,” she whispered, eyes closed, enjoying all the different sensations he was laying on her. She bent her legs to give him more room to navigate inside her as he began to thrust into her, long, slow, languid plunges that hit on her already sensitive flesh and caused sparks of electricity to strobe through her, making her shake and shudder.

“Uuuhhhhh,” she moaned as he began to pick up the pace, watching her face the entire time, noting every tiny reaction.

“Yes baby, come on,” he said as she shivered, fucking into her harder and faster. “Yes…it feels good huh? You like it? You like me fucking you don’t you,” he ground out as his movements became less coordinated. He lifted himself up on his hands so he had more leverage to fuck into her, driving so hard he was pushing her up on the bed until they were flush against the headboard and she spread her hands up to counter the force of his fucking. Allen's eyes rolled into the back of his head as he lost all control, his body taking over to snap his hips into her, rutting into her without ceasing, bodies hot and slick with fluids, the loud slapping of flesh on flesh, alternating with the squelch of wet flesh coming apart and then slamming together again. Frances' mouth was open in an O of utter extremity as her body fell apart beneath her, stuttering and shuddering, wetness spreading everywhere and mixing with Allen's sperm as he came with one last hard thrust into her, body almost bent in two. They collapsed afterward, half blacked out with the intensity of it. The room was silent as soft music continued to play from the speakers.

*****

The day of graduation, they celebrated by staying in bed and fucking each other's brains out. Frances had graduated summa cum laude and Allen had passed his exams. The administrators of the estate had all attended the ceremony and after they'd taken them for lunch at which point they made arrangements with Allen on where and how they would begin the business of transferring his assets wholly into his hands. After lunch, they went home and went to bed and didn't emerge for the next twenty four hours.

"Where are we gonna live after this?" Frances asked. "Will we stay here?"

"No. I think the best place for us is probably New York. You ready for the big time?" he asked caressing her thigh lazily.

Frances shrugged, "I suppose I can write from anywhere." She was already a contributor for an online magazine and had gotten started on her first novel, based on her experience living on the streets.

"Good. Then it's settled," Allen said leaning in to kiss her. she kissed him back and the fire that consumed them every single time their lips touched took over and he was leaning her back into the mattress and climbing on top of her.

"Frannie, my love," he said into the flesh of her neck as he teased it with his tongue.

"Yes," she breathed back, arching her head backward to give him better access and spreading her legs under him so he could get inside her again. She was quite sore from the marathon sex they'd been having but it didn't even occur to her to refuse him. He pushed slowly into her; he had to have been sore too, and then they were moving together, enjoying being so close, so in tune, so in sync with each other that it wasn't even about the sex anymore. It was simply another way for them to be one, a single entity united in love.

*****

New York was a different experience for both of them. It was their first time living in such a huge city and distractions were endless. Allen's job was extroverted, it involved meetings with people and invitations to functions and benefits. Frances was very introverted on the other hand, all she wanted to do was write and be with Allen. They were used to this rhythm though. When Frances came to live with him he was the popular high school kid, and she was the freak who kept to herself and read books. But at the time, they weren't a couple and Allen had been able to go out and have a good time and come back to tell Frances all about it. Now, he pushed her to come with him, he wanted her with him when he went to the functions and benefits and dinners. Frances was not opposed, she wanted to be with him too; but she needed to create a space that was hers, where she was able to write. They compromised; she would accompany him to his functions on the weekends and during the week, he would leave her alone to write. It worked as a compromise until Frances' book came out, and it did well. So well in fact, that she began to get a spot light of her own; she had even less time to devote to Allen because she had her own functions and dinners to attend. Her own galas where she was expected. It was a definite strain on the relationship to have them both pulled in different directions. Frances knew that new compromises would have to be struck, but Allen was opposed to change. He liked the old arrangement, this new one sucked ass.

"Allen we need to talk about this like two adult people," Frances tried once again on the one night they were both home.

"What is there to talk about Frances, you have your shiny new life and you don't need me anymore," he replied.

"That's bullshit and you know it. Why can't you just be reasonable for once?" she asked irritably.

"Oh, I'm unreasonable? *Really*?" he yelled stalking off to get a drink.

"Look, Allen, I don't have time for your immature sulks right now so I'm just gonna go and get some work done," Frances said heading toward her office.

“Oh, I’m too much of a baby for you, am I now? Now that you don’t need me anymore is that it? Fine, I’m leaving,” Allen said slamming down his drink and snatching up his car keys.

“You’re leaving? Where are you going Allen?” she asked changing direction to follow him. He’d had more than one drink already, he wasn’t in any condition to drive.

He stopped to glare at her. “I have options you know. You’re not the only girl in the world,” he bit out.

Frances stared at him. “What does that mean?” she asked in a low voice.

“Figure it out darlin,” he snarled, opening the door and stepping out.

“You want to leave me over some bullshit like this? Okay then, go! Leave!” Frances began pushing Allen until his legs were outside the door. Then she collapsed on the floor and cried until she had no more tears. She didn’t expect that he would try to come back. He was about as mad as she was. It wasn’t her fault; she was trying her best. She couldn’t *help* the fact that her book had suddenly blown up; that she was now as busy as he was. It wasn't her fault they didn't get to spend as much time as they used to together.

It wasn't.

Frances got up, snatched the keys to her jeep and went after him.

Chapter 4

Ambulance sirens, police cars and a crowd of curious onlookers greeted Allen when he turned the car into their street. It looked like there had been some sort of car accident and someone or someones were hurt pretty badly. The police were directing traffic past the wreckage, looked like a white car and a green jeep had-

Allen braked so suddenly, he hit his head on the steering wheel. Thankfully there was no car behind him but the cop was already walking toward him waving his arm to indicate he should keep driving. Allen alighted his vehicle and walked toward the wreckage, heart beating wildly.

"Sir! Sir! I'm going to have to ask you to get back into your car and-" the cop had reached him and was trying to push him back.

"That's my wife's car," Allen heard himself say from a great distance away. The cop abruptly stopped trying to push him.

*****

The other driver was in critical condition; his blood alcohol level was way above the legal limit when he fell asleep at the wheel and careened into Frances reversing out of their driveway. He'd hit the jeep on the right side, where Frances was in the driver's seat and the only thing that had saved her from certain death was that her jeep was much higher than his sports car so he'd hit her low. Still, the damage done was quite enough and Frances lay in a coma, unmoving and unresponsive. The doctors wouldn't let Allen sit with her; something about germs and rest; he wasn't really in the right mind to understand what they were saying. He paced the corridor anxiously, waiting for word on what was happening. "You should go home Mr. St. James, if anything changes, we'll call you," the nurse said kindly to him. He just glared at her and continued to pace. She sighed deeply and walked away, leaving him to his agitation. He realized there was no-one he could call; no-one to lean on. It was just the two of them. And now Frances was lying in a coma.

*****

It was five days and six nights before her eyes fluttered open and she looked around in puzzlement as if wondering where she was. Allen stood up and came to her side, they'd allowed him in the room on the condition that he wore the scrubs and the mask and he'd complied without demur. So all that was visible to her were his piercing gray eyes.

"You're awake," he mumbled through the cloth covering his mouth. The relief in his words was palpable though.

"I'm awake," she repeated in a hoarse voice. "Water?"

He turned quickly to the side table, pouring her a glass from the jug that sat there. He refilled it every three hours on this very off chance, that she would wake up wanting water. He'd seen it in many movies. He picked up a bendy straw and inserted it in the glass and held it to her lips so she could drink. She took a long pull and swallowed; the latter action seemed to be painful for her, and then took another sip.

“Thanks,” she said.

“No problem. I should get the doctor,” he said happily. “Don’t go anywhere.”

“I won’t,” she said as he bounced out of the room.

The doctors and nurses came hurrying in with Allen at the rear, they took her vital signs and tested her reflexes, looked in her eyes and asked her how she was feeling.

“I’m okay,” she said.

“Do you remember what happened?” they asked her.

She stared from one to the other, looking for some clue and then down at herself. “I guess…I was in some sort of… accident?”

The doctor frowned coming forward to shine a light into her eyes again, “What’s your name?”

“Frances Hilton,” she replied at once.

"Good," the doctor said with a smile. "And what year is this Frances?"

Frances stared at him and then at all the other people in the room, lastly her eyes fell on Allen. "Umm, not 2005?" she said.

The excitement in the room dampened considerably.

The doctor's smile disappeared, "What is the last thing you remember Frances?"

Frances hesitated; she really didn't want to say. But everyone was looking at her expectantly.

"I…" she began and then stopped.

"Don't be scared Frances, just tell us the truth," he said.

Frances looked down. "I work for a bookie named Karl; he sent me to collect from a client but the guy attacked me and tried to…" Frances swallowed hard. "I escaped," she finished.

"That must have been before we met," Allen said.

Frances looked up at him. "Who are you?" she asked. All the color drained from Allen's face.

*****

The doctors said it would pass; that retrograde amnesia was fairly common with the injuries she'd suffered. There was nothing to worry about; she would remember. Allen was not so sure; somehow it felt like rejection to him. Why would her amnesia only cover the period where they'd known each other? When he went to see her, she looked at him warily like he was some dangerous stranger. She had asked for her baseball bat the last time he'd been but that weapon had been discarded long ago. He'd given her his pocket knife instead and she'd looked at it in surprise and suspicion before fixing him with a wondering glance. Then she'd slipped it under her pillow with quiet thanks. He hated it. He wanted to scream and rail at her but he couldn't because she was ill. She couldn't help herself. Allen told himself so every day; he still couldn't help feeling like it was some sick revenge for the last thing he'd said to her before he left the apartment that day. He would take it back if he could, she had to know that. But he couldn't even discuss it with her since she didn't remember shit. Allen wasn't sure if that was a blessing or a curse.

"Where do I live?" she asked him when he went to visit the next day.

"With me!" he cried. "You live with me."

"Oh," she said seemingly surprised. "So we're…"

"Together. Yeah," he finished for her.

"Oh," she said again looking down. Her delicate honey complexion was glowing with embarrassment, "I'm sorry I don't remember you."

"Yeah I got that," Allen couldn't quite keep the resentment out of his tone.

There was a small silence.

"The doctors said I could go home tomorrow, that's why I asked," she said softly.

"Uh huh? They didn't tell me," Allen said.

"Well…that's what they said."

"That's good then. Do you need anything in particular; a wheelchair or whatever?" he asked.

Frances smiled wryly. "My head is broken, not my body," she said reminding Allen so poignantly of *his* Frances that he almost burst into tears.

"What?" she asked curiously on seeing his expression.

Allen shook his head, "Nothing. I can't wait for tomorrow."

"Yeah," Frances replied non-committally. "About that…you do know we won't be er…" she asked uncomfortably.

"No, yeah, I got that with the whole 'you don't remember me' thing," he said, sounding a tad bitter.

"I'm sorry," she said sounding irritable herself.

Allen shook his head. "It's not your fault. I'll…be going. Gotta tidy up and what not," he said with a sheepish smile. Frances nodded wondering what he was *really* going to do. Maybe he'd had some other woman stashed in their house that he had to go get rid of.

*****

Allen went running in Central Park. He needed to clear his head and decide what was the best way forward. For one thing, they had not been doing well before her accident, and now she couldn't even remember him. Was it some kind of sign that they should call it quits? And what if Frances wasn't interested in being with him anymore? Like…ever? It wasn't like they had much in common beyond their shared history. He was all about people and she lived inside her head. She was all book smart and long talks about abstract concepts while he was all about sports and music and parties. It didn't bode well for their future together if she didn't remember *why* they even got together in the first place. It was a cluster fuck any way he looked at it and he didn't know if he wanted to stick around for the blow back. Still, she had nowhere else to go for now, and nobody else to turn to; so he guessed he would just have to do.

*****

She was impressed by the size of their house. She knew he was rich because she had a private room in the hospital and the staff treated her special. She knew it wasn't her because there was no way she'd gone from Karl's collector to a multimillionaire in such a short time. She'd looked at herself in the mirror and she didn't look any older than 25. She didn't ask what the date was though, or the year. It was too much to think about, missing all those years of her life. It was like waking up after being roofied in a strange bed, with no idea if you were there voluntarily or without consent. Of course if someone had roofied her, it was unlikely that she was there voluntarily. But no one had roofied her; she'd been in an accident, hit her head, and lost her memory. Clearly, that Allen guy cared enough for her to hang out at the hospital while she was out cold, and he'd been to see her every day since. There was just something about him…she didn't know what but she guessed he was mad at her for some reason. Or mad at something. Or maybe that was just his character. How would *she* know?

“It's nice here,” she said.

“Yeah, well you decorated most of it so it makes sense that you would like it.”

“I did? Wow, I have good taste,” she said looking around.

Allen laughed. “I guess you do. So about bedrooms…we have three plus the master. Do you want to keep it or you wanna move out?” he asked.

“I want to do what’s the least disruptive thing,” she said looking at him.

“The least disruptive thing would be to maintain the status quo but that’s off the table so…” Allen said.

Frances sighed. She wanted to tell him he was being an immature asshole but she didn’t know him well enough to say such a thing; or rather, apparently she did but she didn’t remember. She wondered how they’d gotten together. He was clearly very Will Smith while she was more Tupac Shakur. What the hell did they even have in common?

“Okay then, I’ll move to one of the guest rooms for now. How about that?” she proposed.

Allen shrugged but said nothing, just looked at her from beneath his eyelashes and walked down the hall to what she assumed was the master. She followed him, looking around their room. The bed was neatly made, with an off white duvet; a gray sheet peeking out from under it. The pillows were gaily patterned with red roses on a white background. The whole thing was very cozy and she could imagine burrowing in there with a guy on cold nights, just enjoying being warm. She could remember clearly all the cold winter nights she’d shivered through in her bunker. Clearly those days were far behind her but in her current state, they were pretty immediate.

“This is a pretty room,” she said.

“Yeah,” he agreed.

“Lemme guess, I decorated it too?” she asked.

Allen smiled, “We both did.”

Frances took a deep breath, “I have a proposal,” she said.

“Uh huh?” Allen seemed very aloof.

“I was thinking about what the doctor said about doing things that might be familiar to jog my memory. So maybe I ought to stay in here…with you,” she said, unable to stop the color from suffusing her cheeks.

Allen’s face brightened, “I’m okay with that.”

“But no sex or nothin,” Frances hastened to add.

Allen put his hands up to show how harmless he was, “Of course, yeah.”

Frances breathed in deeply, “Great. That’s good. So what’s next on the agenda? I’m kinda hungry.”

Allen laughed, “Yeah okay, this way to the kitchen. I think I can rustle up some sandwiches before dinner.”

“Thank you,” she said.

“Why don’t you…relax, maybe look around and get your bearings while I get that sandwich?” he suggested.

“Good idea,” Frances agreed, taking a step toward the bed. She wanted to see if it was as soft as it looked. Knowing her, if she’d had a chance, she’d have chosen the softest bed in existence. She sat down on it, all her expectations coming to fruition as it enveloped her in luxurious softness.

“Aaahh,” she sighed in contentment, flopping back on the bed and spreading her arms out. The bed was huge, even if she slept with Allen, there was enough space that they didn’t have to even touch each other if they didn’t want to. Frances closed her eyes, luxuriating in comfort.

“You fell asleep,” a voice startled her awake. She sat up quickly, scrambling around for her baseball bat before she remembered where she was.

“It's okay, you’re fine,” Allen said standing in the doorway holding a plate. Frances just stared at him, trying to shake the instinctive panic that still curled her fingers around a non-existent weapon. He walked toward her, holding the plate of sandwiches out like an offering.

“Here’s your food,” he said.

“Thanks,” she whispered hoarsely and moved from the bed to the chair to eat her sandwich. She didn’t want to get crumbs on the perfect bed. She ate in silence while Allen sat on the bed and watched her. It was awkward but she couldn’t think of anything to say and apparently he couldn’t be bothered. She finished her meal and then looked up at him and smiled.

“So,” she said. “Tell me about me.”

Allen smiled. “Aren’t you supposed to wait for your memory to return naturally?”

Frances shrugged. “Maybe, but I’d like to hear the highlights anyway. Especially the dirty laundry. For example, why are we together?”

“That’s dirty laundry?” Allen’s eyebrows almost disappeared into his hair.

“I don’t know, do I? How did we meet?” she asked leaning forward. A wave of nausea overtook her and she had to lean back again, “Ooh.”

“What’s wrong?” Allen asked standing up as she put one hand to her head and the other to her stomach.

“I don’t know,” Frances said. Then she stood up very suddenly and ran to the bathroom. She got to the toilet just in time for her sandwich to come pouring savagely out, as well as the contents of her saline drip at the hospital and any bile that might have accumulated. After that it was any air left in her esophagus and finally the heaving stopped.

“What was that?” she asked very perturbed as she wiped her mouth.

“I don’t know,” Allen said slowly. “Maybe we should call the doctor.”

Frances shook her head, “No, it's fine, I’m feeling okay now, we don’t have to call anyone.”

Allen shrugged, “If you say so…shall I make you another sandwich?”

“Er, yeah if you don’t mind.”

"I don't mind. Just go lie down and I'll be right back." Allen hurried out of the room as she watched. She crossed over to the bed and sat on it, ignoring the burning in her stomach in favor of enjoying the softness. She figured she'd probably been sleeping in this bed long enough to take it all for granted, but not long enough to have forgotten the hard floor and the barely there mattress; the funky smell of the bunker, the cold, wet, hunger…sure it was however many years ago it had been, but in her head, it might as well have been yesterday. The discomfort of nausea could hardly compare to the memory of all that.

Allen came in carrying another sandwich with a glass of juice and some salad on the side. He really was a handsome fellow, and those eyes were to die for. She just didn't see how they *fit*.

"The cook's arrived," he said grinning at her.

She smiled back out of politeness, "Great." She took the plate from him, studying its contents. The nausea seemed to have disappeared so she ate with gusto and finished her meal. She held her breath for a few minutes, wondering if the vomiting would begin again but this time the food stayed down.

"Huh..." she said. "Maybe my body just needed a salad."

Allen laughed, "Maybe." He breathed in deep, "Soo, do you wanna watch a movie or something?"

"Er, how about some entertainment news? I'd like to see who is popular now."

Allen laughed, "Since when do you care about such shit?"

Frances shrugged, "Hey, it's the fastest way to catch up."

"Catch up on what?"

"On what people find important," she said.

"Don't you wanna know what *you've* been up to?"

"Oh. Wow. Do I wanna know?" she asked wincing in anticipation.

Allen smiled, "Yes, you really do."

"Tell me tomorrow. I think I need a bath and rest for now."

"You're the boss," Allen said standing up to leave her to it.

The next morning when she woke, Frances vomited again. Allen pulled rank and declared they were going to the doctor whether she liked it or not.

Chapter 5

"You're pregnant," the doctor declares baldly, coming into the room and placing the results of the tests in front of them.

Frances stared at him in shock.

"No I'm not," she stated.

"I'm afraid you are. We've done all the tests from MRI to UTI and that's what came back," the doctor replied. They had indeed done what was seemingly every test known to man. They had been at the hospital all day doing them. They took blood, urine, spinal fluid…it had been nerve wracking. Frances almost felt cheated that all they'd found was a baby. *A baby! Oh my God, I'm having a baby!*

Frances could feel the hysteria building and building. She was ready to run away screaming. She glanced at Allen, sitting woodenly next to her. His face was impassive, whatever he was feeling was hidden deep inside. Frances felt her breathing escalate, she would be hyperventilating in a minute if she wasn't careful. The doctor was gabbing on, something about options; abortion was mentioned. Allen seemed to be listening intently, taking it all in. He would have to fill her in later, once her ears stopped ringing. She looked from Allen to the doctor, seeing little pin pricks of light in front of them. *Was she seeing stars?* Suddenly, her vision went black and she knew no more.

*****

"Frances! Fran! Frannie girl you better wake up now and stop fucking around," the voice was yelling in her ear and she turned her face to get away from it. It sounded terrified which was weird; what was there to be terrified about? Slowly, she opened her eyes and looked around. She was lying on something soft and a white coated gentleman was standing a few feet away. The guy who'd been there when she woke up was looming over her, his black curly hair falling into his terrified gray eyes. He really had the most amazing eyes she'd ever seen. He was saying something to her, sounding either annoyed or scared, she couldn't really tell which. She felt dizzy and discombobulated. Her hand rose to close over his arm.

“What’s happening?” she asked him, trying to remember what his name was.

“You fainted,” he replied definitely sounding annoyed now.

“Oh,” she said hazily. “That sounds unlikely, I don’t faint.”

“Well, you just did,” he snapped.

“What was your name again?” she asked eyes drifting to his face. His red, annoyed face.

“Allen St. James,” he bit out. “I’m practically your husband so I’ll thank you to remember it.”

“How’d I snag you anyway? Was it a love potion?” she asked. She felt a little drunk…I mean, how she assumed people felt when they were drunk. She couldn’t really remember.

Allen laughed, his face lightening considerably. “You adopted me,” he said cryptically. She frowned at him, waiting for further explanation but he said nothing. The doctor took a step forward.

“Mr. St. James in light of current events, I think it would be prudent to admit Ms. Hilton overnight,” he said.

“I’m right here,” Frances said not liking the way he was talking over her. He turned toward her with an apologetic smile.

“I’m sorry Ms. Hilton, I didn’t mean to leave you out of the discussion,” he said.

“Forgiven. So why do you need to observe me overnight?”

“Well given your accident and subsequent injuries, and now with the pregnancy and the fainting, we need to check that everything is fine, that your body is healthy enough for this, identify the reason behind the fainting; perhaps you’re anemic; nothing showed up in the blood tests but we can’t be too careful.

“Maybe it was just shock? I’m pretty sure it was,” Frances said.

“Yeah, it could be that. In fact, given the circumstances, most likely that’s what it is. But we can’t take the risk of taking that for granted.”

“Fine. I’ll stay the night,” even to her own ears, Frances sounded sulky. Allen smiled.

“It’s a good thing. Give us some time to get used to the new status quo and what not,” he said.

She looked at him with a side smile. “Well, can I have a computer? I noticed that we had some in the apartment.”

Allen laughed. “Sure you can, especially since it's yours. Did you er, wanna do some writing?”

“Writing?” Frances asked uncertainly.

“Yeah, you’re a writer,” he said. He sounded quite proud of her. her internal eyebrow rose to see it.

“Am I any good?” she asked. Allen laughed.

“Tell you what, I’ll bring you the book you wrote and you can judge for yourself.”

“I wrote a book?!? Don’t you think you should have led with that?” she asked voice going high with shock.

“Sorry,” Allen said not sounding at all apologetic. “Everything’s been crazy. It wasn’t exactly in the front of my mind.”

Frances fell back; he did have a point. “Okay then. Well…I'll just check in and you can go…bring the stuff.”

“I'll do that. See you,” he said looking at her expectantly as if she was meant to do something with that.

“Bye,” she said with a small wave hoping it would suffice. She turned around to follow the doctor to her room for the night, she knew Allen was watching her go and put a little sway in her step. She didn't know why but she wanted him to be attracted to her. *She* was attracted to *him*…it was strange; it had snuck up on her when she wasn't looking. Maybe that was what had happened before and she had seduced him? Sooner or later she needed to get him to tell her how they met.

The nurses got her settled in and she promptly went to sleep waking only when someone came to take her blood or other fluids or check her temperature or pressure readings. She hadn't realized she was so tired until she let herself just relax and drop off. When she woke up much later, she saw that Allen had been and gone. A laptop sat on the bedside table and on top of it was a book. There was also an overnight bag sitting on the chair but Allen himself was nowhere to be seen. He probably had to go off and come to terms with the whole, 'We're having a baby' thing too. She picked up the book and studied it.

Confessions of a Former Street Urchin

By Frances Hilton

Based on a True Story

The cover said. There was a picture of a cutsie little urchin on the cover. Some publisher's interpretation of Frances' own untidy haired intransigence she guessed. She stared at her name on the cover, fascinated to see her name on the cover of a book. Turned out that all those stories she used to keep under her mattress actually amounted to something. She turned the book over to see the back cover. A picture of her looking sophisticated, hair combed, actual make up on her face, stared back at her with a smug smile. She read the blurb at the back. The book was supposed to be about her life as she saw it. How convenient. She leaned back on the pillow and opened the first page, hoping her own book wasn't going to bore her to death. She made herself comfortable and began to read.

*****

Allen came for her the next morning and she looked at him with new eyes. It seemed they had come from far together. The doctor gave them some anti-nausea pills to go home with as well as advising them to keep an eye on Frances' blood pressure. He also gave them various pamphlets about pregnancy, adoption and abortion. Frances took them but didn't look at them, just followed Allen out of the hospital. He didn't drive straight home; instead he took her to an ice cream parlor and sat her at one of the window tables as he went to get their orders. He didn't ask her what she wanted so she guessed she either had a particular preference every time or he was just that overbearing. The jury was out on which it was. He came back with peppermint chocolate ice-cream for her, and a vanilla one for himself. She tasted hers, and found that it was delicious so maybe this was the one she ordered every time. She pondered for a moment whether it was worth asking about but then decided they probably had more serious things to discuss. They'd skirted the issue for long enough and it didn't look like Allen was about to bring it up. So Frances would have to.

"So…about the baby," she began after taking a deep breath.

"Yeah, about that," Allen agreed.

"What are we going to do?" she asked.

"Wow, I was hoping you would tell *me,*" he said with a laugh.

"Oh, so I'm like the Monica in this relationship?" she asked.

"The Monica as in…?" Allen asked.

"As in Monica and Chandler."

Allen laughed, "Not really. We're more Phoebe and Mike."

Frances smiled. "Well that's a relief. But back to the question at hand, what are we doing about the fact that we're having a freaking baby?"

“Frankly, I’m surprised it hasn’t happened before; we’ve been kinda careless in the past. But of course it *would* happen now, at the most awkward time in all humanity.”

“Is it something that we would have wanted? You know… before?” she asked looking intently into his eyes.

Allen looked away and didn’t say anything.

“I’m guessing no…” Frances concluded.

Allen shrugged, “It's been a tricky time.”

“We’re not in a good place huh?”

“That’s one way of putting it.”

“And that’s why you’ve been so distant,” she concluded. Allen looked at her in surprise.

“How would you know that? Have you remembered something?” he asked, eyes hopeful.

Frances looked regretful. “I wish. No, I just figured there was no way we could be like…the way we are. Plus I read the book; we’re portrayed as a lot closer than we seem now.”

“Well, right now, one person doesn’t remember the other so it’d be a bit awkward to be close.”

“I get you, but I get the feeling you’re mad at me. Could we possibly talk about *that*?”

“Sure. You wrote a book, you blew up. Your life got busy. You didn’t have time for me anymore.”

“Oh, so totally all my fault?” Frances said with a smirk.

“Well, I was a pretty sulky big baby about it so I’m guessing that didn’t help,” he conceded.

“Look at you! Growin up and shit…” she said punching him lightly in the shoulder.

“Yeah, look at me,” Allen repeated dryly.

“Anyway, so…now that I don’t remember my writing career, do we still got a problem?” she asked.

Allen shrugged. “I don’t know. I don’t need you to be unhappy so we can be good, okay? I just need you to make some time for me.”

“That sounds reasonable. Especially since I don’t know you from Adam but I don’t know anyone else either so-“

Her phone rang and she looked down at it in surprise. “Who is…Kareemshe?” she asked Allen. He grimaced and sighed. “He’s your ex-boyfriend who is turning into a chick,” he said. She stared at him with her mouth open, “Say what now?” Allen pointed at the phone, “You going to answer it?” he asked. Frances snatched up the phone, having totally forgotten that she's supposed to answer when the phone rings.

“H-hallo?” she said.

“Hey gowrrl, where have you been? So quiet. Are we in a fight?”

“What? No we’re not in a fight. I’d have to remember you for us to be in a fight,” she said unthinkingly.

“Ouch,” Kareemshe said.

“I mean, I’m sorry, didn’t you hear? I had an accident, I have amnesia,” she hastened to say before Kareemshe became offended. Her friend burst into laughter.

“You’re so funny Fran, I swear it's one of the things I love about you.”

“Er...” Frances said awkwardly, not knowing if she should ask about the ‘I love about you’ part…was that purely in a platonic way or…?

“I’m actually dead serious,” she said at last.

There was silence on the line.

“Hallo?” Frances said looking at the screen to see if Kareemshe had hung up.

“You’re serious?” Kareemshe asked.

“Yes. I’m serious. I have amnesia. I don’t know you Kareemshe,” she said. Allen covered his eyes and winced and she looked at him with raised eyebrows.

“Its just Kareem,” he whispered to her. Frances’ mouth dropped open as she realized she’d put her foot in it.

“Sorry, I meant Kareem. Ummm, do you want to maybe come over and visit?” she asked to make up for her rudeness.

“I would, if I wasn’t all the way here in *Vegas,*” she/he said. “Tell that no-good man of yours I’m not amused that he didn’t tell me about this.”

“I’ll pass on the message. Vegas huh? Sounds fun.”

“Hmmm, it's okay. They don’t care about what sex I am over here as long as I pull my weight in the shows.”

“And you’re fine with that?” Frances asked not really knowing what to say but not wanting to lose a friend if that was what Kareemshe was.

“Yeah. I have a holiday coming up in the next two weeks. Maybe I’ll come out there,” she/he said.

“That’s cool. Will you er, stay with us? I’m pretty sure we have enough space.”

Kareemshe laughed, “I guess you really do have amnesia. I’ll see you next week and we can catch up.”

"Okay…bye," Frances said and waited for Kareemshe's reply before she hung up.

She glared at Allen. "Do I have any other friends you neglected to inform of my condition?"

Allen shrugged. "I was distracted," he said simply. There was something in his eyes though, when he said it; as if he'd been in far much more distress than he was letting on. This situation was so complicated and now there was a baby.

"Are we ever going to talk about the baby?" she asked.

"It takes nine months to grow one, right? We have time."

Frances lifted her brow, "That is assuming we aren't getting rid of it."

Allen leaned forward on the table, "Do you *want* to get rid of it?"

Frances thought about it seriously, vague memories of her mother leaving her alone to fend for herself when she could barely understand what that meant, and her vow, made silently but no less resolutely, that a child of hers would *never* go through that. She looked at Allen with his thousand dollar watch and his entitled attitude; would he let his child rot on the street? Somehow she didn't think so. She knew *she* wouldn't let her child fall by the wayside like that.

"I don't think I do," she said at last.

"Well then, I guess we do have nine months to decide where to go from here."

"Just one question, if we were fighting so much, when did we have the time to have unprotected sex?" she asked.

Allen smiled, "Make up sex is the best kind."

*****

It had been a Tuesday, Allen remembered clearly because he'd had a full day at the office and he was tired as shit. Mondays were his day off…the weekends were technically not work days but there was always some work-related soiree, benefit, golf tournament, or other event that he had to attend that he pretty much thought of weekends as socializing work days. But Mondays…Mondays were just for him. He stayed home, he hassled Frances so she had to stop whatever she was doing and goof around with him, he cooked for them, they watched movies or stayed in bed all afternoon…it was usually wonderful.

That Monday though, Frances had been busy; some book thing that had been suddenly rescheduled from the weekend. So Allen had been…out of sorts. The negativity in the house had spilled over into Tuesday and when he had come home, he'd found Frances in the kitchen, arms crossed, ready for battle.

"How long am I going to be on double secret probation?" she'd asked glaring at him.

"I don't know what you're talking about," he said crossing over to the wine bar to pour himself a whiskey. He was too sober for this conversation.

"I'm talking about the fact that you sulk every time I go out for some book function and I just want to know if that's a permanent situation or something you plan to get over some time soon."

Allen poured a second glass of whiskey and kept silent.

"What? You stonewalling me now Al? Me?" Frances demanded.

"I'm not stonewalling anyone Frannie Fran, I'm drinking my whiskey and avoiding an argument."

"You'd do better to avoid an argument by not sulking in the first place," Frances bit out.

Allen turned around suddenly, slamming his glass down on the counter so the liquid jumped and spilled. "Fine. I'm sorry I was 'sulking' or whatever. I'll try to be happy to not spend any time with you from now on."

"Oh, grow up," Frances replied in irritation and stalked off down the hall to their room. Allen took a breath to steady his rapidly rising ire and followed her. He slammed the bedroom door after he walked in, startling her and making her spin around to face him in surprise.

“What?” she got out before he was on her like a shark swallowing its prey. He propelled her backward onto the bed and they both fell, Allen stretching his hands out to break his fall so that he wouldn’t fall on her.

“Shut up,” he said, even though she wasn’t exactly trying to talk. His lips came down and fastened onto hers, the caress more angry than tender. Frances wrapped her arms around his neck and pulled him in anyway, softening in a way that let him know she yielded, she submitted to him; whatever he wanted, he could have. He didn’t even have to ask. Well, what he wanted was all of it, all of her, all the time. It was all consuming, this feeling in his chest that caused him to rip her clothes from her body with controlled savagery and bite at her lip just so he could mark her, everyone would know who she belonged to for weeks to come. Her delicate honey complexion showed every bruise for as long as it took to heal. The site of the redness on her lip was like a red flag to a bull. Allen’s vision went hazy and he tore at his fly, not really coordinated enough to get them off efficiently. Then her hands were on him and he took his own away, letting her relieve him of his jeans and his shirt and his boxers. He stood naked and trembling before her as she leaned in and licked a line up his painfully hard penis. He shivered in reaction and snapped his hips forward, seeking the warmth of her mouth even as she moved away. She got on her knees and took off her shirt which was hanging half on, half off her. Her eyes were steady on him as he took in her body.

“Frannie,” he growled taking a step forward and putting one knee on the bed.

“Al,” she breathed in reply, leaning forward to place her lip on the side of his mouth, tongue peeking out to taste. “Fuck me,” she whispered as she took his ear between her teeth.

“Uh,” he groaned as he circled her waist with his hands and threw her backward so she fell sprawled onto the bed, legs spread wide. “Fran,” he whispered as he covered her body with his, penetrating her in one long thrust as his breath caught in his chest and he literally felt his heart stop. Her legs came up as she held onto them with her hands, giving him full access to her wet warmth. Hips snapping with vigor and speed, he rutted into her; mouth open and breath coming fast and hard and hoarse. His eyes rolled to the back of his head as he listened to the sounds she was making; full of want and lust and *need*. Allen's stomach hurt with the need to be deep inside her and he doubled his efforts, the friction creating an impossible heat that fueled the fires of his passion.

"Fran," he bit out, his lungs empty of oxygen as he forgot to breath. Her hands let go of her legs which wrapped themselves around his middle as her hands inched up to tangle with his. Her back arched propelling him even deeper into her as she moaned, eyes fluttering as her internal muscles shivered with sensitivity. He thrust harder into her, reaching down to capture her lips as he felt his orgasm bearing down on him.

“Come with me,” he murmured as he fucked deeper and deeper into her. She made a sound somewhere between pain and pleasure, threw her head back and shuddered into her completion. He let himself go as she did, happy to be in sync with her at least in this *one* thing. He collapsed on top of her, breathing hard, not bothering to remove his weight from her chest for a moment. Too fucked out to care how heavy he was. She uttered no word of protest so Allen assumed she was too well fucked to care too. Eventually though, he moved to the side, leaving his hand around her as his head found that hollow in her neck to nestle into.

“I love you,” he murmured, his version of apology.

“Yeah, I know. I love you too,” she replied. “Just sometimes, I'm not sure I *like* you.”

Allen laughed, “You like me just fine. You just can't remember it when you're annoyed.”

Frances smiled. “Touché,” she said closing her eyes.

“So…friends again?” he asked sleepily.

“Best Friends,” she replied dropping of to sleep.

Three weeks’ later, she’d been in an accident, reversing out of their driveway.

Chapter 6

Hey Kareem, according to my book we're pretty close so I have something to ask you. When you get this message could you call me back?

Frances hit the send button and then sat back on her chair. She was in her study, spying on her own life through her laptop. She'd looked at her Facebook page, which had mostly writing-related stuff and a lot of photos of her and Allen all dressed up attending various things. Or herself alone attending various things. Her updates were funny, sarcastic and self deprecating; it looked like, online anyway, she had it all together. Her twitter was even more work-related with announcements of various locations where she'd be doing book signings and appearances. There were a few personal posts, also funny or self deprecating. Very few of them had anything to do with her actual life. She sighed, resolving to go make some coffee and think about more important matters...

like the constant, 24/7 nausea that was assailing her life right now; or the fact that she and Allen were living in limbo thanks to her memory loss. Her phone went off, taking her out of her head for a bit.

“Girl, whatchu goin through?” Kareem’s voice said.

“I’m just…I’m pregnant,” she blurted out and held her breath for his/her reaction.

“What?” Kareem yelled into her receiver, making her move the phone as far from her ear as it could go.

“From that reaction, I take it this isn’t good news?” she said when the echo had dissipated.

“No! Of course it's…it's just that…I…I mean it's great,” he stuttered to a stop at last.

“Like…seriously? Could you sound less devastated about it then?”

“I’m sorry. It's just that…” Kareem sighed. “Babies are so permanent.”

“And this relationship isn’t right?” she finished for him.

“What makes you say that?” Kareem asked at once.

“I figured that was what you meant,” Frances said.

“No, I just, God Fran, I’m still in love with you, you know that,” he said in a defeated tone.

“What? Really? No, I didn’t fucking know that. It didn’t say that in my book,” she protested, completely thrown by this confession. “Is this something you and I like…talk about or…?” Her breathing was coming hard and fast. Just what kind of tangled up love life did she *have*?

“Nah, of course we don’t talk about it. I mean I made a choice and so did you. We live with the consequences.”

“It sounds so complicated, why are we such good friends then?”

“Because that’s all we can be,” Kareem said.

“So…if you weren’t…and *I* wasn’t…” Frances stuttered.

“Naw...Allen always came first with you. Even when we were together…” Kareem sighed.

"But…I didn't cheat on you or nothin did I?" she asked afraid of the answer.

"No, of course not. You were the best girlfriend a guy could ask for."

"Well…that's a relief," Frances said with a laugh. "In light of that though, you still wanna come spend some time with us? Maybe add to the awkwardness factor in my life a little?"

"Baby, I can't wait," he said and she could hear the smile in his voice.

"Well…good. Because you seem like a really good guy."

"Unlike Allen you mean?"

"That is not what I said," Frances protested.

"You don't need to front for me girl, I know you."

Frances sighed, "I just…I'm having a hard time figuring him out. One moment he is wildly attractive, the next he's just such a jackass. And then there's the whole 'I'm pregnant' thing so I don't know if it's that messing with my mind or it's the amnesia or it's just Allen."

“Probably all three?” Kareem suggested.

Frances sighed, “Hurry up and come to town Kareem. I really wanna meet you.”

“I will. Hold on okay? It's just another week.”

“Okay, I will,” Frances said.

“Bye girlfriend,” Kareem said softly.

“Bye…boygirlfriend,” Frances replied making Kareem laugh. She felt a lot better after that conversation though and decided to look at her draft folder to see what she was working on. Maybe she still had writing skills. She could hear the chef pottering about in the kitchen. She really wanted a sandwich but she was afraid to go and ask him to make one, or to do it herself lest he be offended. He looked like a really uppity sort. If she didn’t get something inside her soon though, she might just start eating out her stomach…

She stood up and crept to the kitchen, peering around the wall to see what the chef was up to. There was a plate on the kitchen island. On the plate was a steak, some salad and a huge baked potato. Frances could feel her mouth water just looking at it.

“Are you going to have your lunch now or not?” the chef said not looking at her.

“Er…is that mine?” she asked tentatively.

The chef looked around in an exaggerated way. “Do you see anyone else around here?” he asked. Frances wanted to say that ‘yeah, I see you’, but she didn’t quite have the nerve. She walked slowly forward and picked up the plate, covering it with her other hand as if someone was attempting to take food from her plate. She walked into the living room, plopped on the chair and switched on the TV; watching some entertainment channel as she ate. As far as she could tell, pop culture had gone to shit while she was forgettin’ it in the hospital. Who the fuck were these Kardashians and why were they everywhere?

She fell asleep after lunch and woke to Allen shaking her.

“Hi,” he said smiling down at her.

“Hi,” she replied looking up at him with raised brows.

“You’re not answering your phone. I got three calls from your book people asking me panicked questions so I thought I’d come and find out if anything was the matter. Since you weren’t picking up *my* calls either,” he was smiling as he said it though so Frances figured she wasn’t in trouble.

“I didn’t hear the phone. Must have really slept deep,” she said.

“Yeah, and your phone was in your office,” Allen said holding it up.

“Should I call them back now?” she asked.

“Nah. Tomorrow is soon enough; I told them you were still in no condition to be bothered. They weren’t happy.”

“What do they want from me?” she asked shifting her legs off the couch so he could sit beside her.

Allen shrugged, sat down and put her legs in his lap, massaging her feet. “I’m guessing they need to reschedule your missed dates or something,” he said eyes on her feet. He was making electric shocks shoot up her legs to her center. Just from massaging her feet. Who knew.

“Great. I mean, not great. Do they know I’m pregnant and nauseous?” she asked.

Allen shook his head and then looked up at her face, “Unless *you* told them?”

“Nope, don’t even know who they are,” she said.

“Okay, so they don’t know. I guess we can call them tomorrow and I can help you where I can,” he said.

“Don’t you like…have work to do?” she asked hesitantly.

“I can work from here, and I have a myriad of assistants and lackeys and minions to do my bidding when I’m not there. Don’t even sweat it,” he said with a wave of his hand.

“Well…good then, I could really use the help. Sometimes all this seems so overwhelming.”

“I know; I mean, I don’t know but I can imagine that it's not easy for you. And you’ve been taking it like a champ. I just wanna tell you that I'm gonna look after you and we're going to be alright," he said.

She stared at him. "Okay…thanks," she said slowly.

He shook his head. "Don't thank me. I owe you," he said.

"What do you owe me?" she asked puzzled.

"My life? My sanity? Everything?" he said with a small laugh.

Frances put her chin on her knuckle. "That's rather vague," she said narrowing her eyes at him and causing him to laugh out loud.

"You've read your book right?"

She nodded her head.

"So you know that you literally picked me up off the street?"

"Yeah, that's what it said. I wasn't sure how true that was. You really *were* a street kid?"

"For a few days, before you met me and rescued me. I'd probably be dead now if it wasn't for you."

"But…you had a home to go to," she said in puzzlement.

"Yeah well..." Allen shrugged. "Anyway, my point is it's probably time to balance the scales and pay you back for taking such epic care of me all of these years."

"I think you already did that. You brought me back to live with you when the police found you, right? Took *me* off the street? Paid my tuition?"

"It was selfish. You were the only person in my life who liked me for me rather than what I had."

"You can't know that. Not for sure."

Allen smiled. "And that's exactly why I can," he said cryptically then stood up. "I want some coffee. Do you want some coffee?" he asked as he walked to the kitchen. Frances got up on her knees, leaning on the back of the sofa to watch him go. "The Chef's still in there," she whispered frantically at him as he headed to the kitchen. Allen turned to smile at her.

"So?" he asked.

"I don't think he likes people just going in there," she said.

Allen laughed out loud and then disappeared around the corner. Frances sighed and sat back down waiting to hear the explosion. Nothing happened for a time and then Allen was back with coffee. He wasn't alone.

"Frannie? Meet Miguel; he's our cook. You and he get along very well. Like a house on fire," he said as if he was speaking to a kid. Miguel stepped forward and held both hands out to her.

"Ms. Hilton, I am sorry for your troubles," he said taking both hands into his and kissing first one then the other.

"Oh," Frances said unable to process or even think of a single thing to say.

He put her hands down in her lap, bowed to her and disappeared back into the kitchen. Frances watched him go with her mouth open.

"Okay. So I've been skulking all day for no reason?" she asked. Allen laughed.

"I guess you have. Did you want anything else from the kitchen?"

"Well…I could eat," she said with a twist of her lips.

"Miguel!" Allen called making Frances wince; so rude.

The cook came back round the corner, "Yes, Mr. Allen."

"Frances would like some food," Allen said.

"Ah, I have some nice carrots and tomatoes, maybe some cheese? I could make a nice salad," he suggested.

"Okay, that sounds good but could I have something with that, maybe some French fries? A hot dog…?"

Allen laughed, "Shall I order some pizza instead; sounds like you want some serious junk food."

"Pizza sounds good," Frances brightened then she turned to face Miguel. "Not that I don't appreciate the salad; I'll eat that too," she pacified.

Miguel smiled, "How about I bring the salad and *then* make you a pizza?"

Frances bowed to him, "You are a man among men Miguel."

*****

Frances seemed to see saw between hunger and nausea. One seemed to always precipitate the other; it was a never ending circle of misery. She was surprised at how patient Allen was with her. He began going to work in the morning only, spending his afternoons with her. She'd canceled her speaking engagements because she wasn't confident about being able to pull that off. But she figured she could do book signings; she could still sign her name after all and at least she was sure of what it was. She was having a hard time accepting that she was a published author popular enough to *have* these problems; either way, she was grateful.

When they came home from these functions, Allen would rub her feet and baby her and make her feel like a princess and when they went to bed, he said 'goodnight' and turned his back on her, dropping off to sleep with apparently no problem. Frances was having trouble sleeping though. All the attention, the massages, the flirting, the eye contact; it got her all heated up and she was all primed up with nowhere to go. She wondered if it was pregnancy hormones making her so horny or was it just Allen? She didn't feel like she could talk to him about it because for all she knew, he was feeling absolutely nothing about this whole messed up situation. Sure he was attentive and loving…but maybe it was because he felt he owed her rather than any interest he had in jumping her bones. I mean, what kind of guy had this much self-control? They slept in the same bed every night and he didn't so much as cop a feel. It was humiliating.

She turned around to face him, tracing the length of his broad back with her eyes. Her hand trailed downward, past her stomach to caress the downy hair that covered her center. Tiny tendrils of sensation suffused her stomach with warmth as a finger moved downward and inward, seeking the wetness of her entrance. She was leaking like a faulty faucet and it was all Allen's fault. He lay in front of her, back moving slowly as he breathed in and out; he was already asleep? Her finger pressed harder, going in deeper, finding that sensitive nub and rubbing it gently as she closed her eyes and imagined it was Allen's finger seeking inside of her. Pretty soon, a finger began to feel inadequate and she added a second one, imagining it was Allen getting on top of her, penis hard and ready and pressing into her with lust and desire, whispering her name into her ear as he bit into her neck. His breath exhaling in relief, completion and desire as he drove himself home at last. Then he would withdraw and thrust again, seeking the sensitive places inside her, making electrical impulses shoot every which way; her back would arch just the way it wanted to do now; but she couldn't because she might wake him. Instead, she spread her legs wider, controlling her breathing with difficulty as she felt that balloon of feeling build inside her; she wanted it to be him so bad she almost reached out her hand to touch his back, to ask for this one thing; it didn't have to mean anything. This was basic, feral need; she needed a dick inside of her and he had one. She felt the release come at the thought and she couldn't resist jerking a bit as her eyesight dimmed for a minute, hand weakening with the aftershocks. She slumped back on the pillow and watched Allen's back, caressing him with her eyes before they closed and she slept.

*****

'Did she just fucking masturbate right in front of me?'

Allen *wasn't* asleep; in fact he was very awake, very hard and in pain. He'd been persuading himself to drift off, had almost managed it in fact when he felt it; her breathing had changed; become more harsh. She was moving very subtly on the bed but he didn't mistake those sounds, however quiet she tried to be…How many times had they made love over the years? A hundred? A hundred thousand? He knew how she sounded when she was aroused; he knew her sex sounds. And she was definitely making them right now. His body was conditioned to respond to those sounds, the smell emanating from her; a subtle musk that awakened the Casanova in him, made him come out to play. Now, here he was, all dolled up with nowhere to go. He'd been trying so hard to give her space, make her comfortable, be the grown up for once…and this is how she repaid him? With teasing reminders of what he knew they had and she apparently didn't? Allen heard her breathing even out and a tiny snore issued from her nose. So he knew she was asleep when he reached down and began to tug himself. It hurt a bit so he looked on the counter to see if there was any lotion nearby. It would be too much of a give away to walk to the bathroom right now and Frances was a light sleeper.

He shoved his pajamas aside making room for his hand, moaning very quietly as it caught on his hard on. He imagined Frances's hand pulling them down, her soft hands brushing across his erection. It all made him want to moan and buck his hips wildly for more. But he couldn't because then she would hear and truly understand the extent of his sickness.

"That's my Allen so hot and all for me."

Allen closed his eyes as he imagined Frances's face, her lips all moist and plump for the taking. He leaned back on the sheets and grasped his hard on, softly stroking himself from base to head.

"Oooh you like that Allen? Like my hand on your dick?" imaginary Frances said in his head.

"Ye-sss....God, *yeeeeessss"* He whispered soundlessly as he played with the slit, smearing pre-come on and around the head paying extra attention to the thready vein that was pulsing hard and fast. Allen stuttered and removed his right hand from his dick and placed his fingers in his mouth lubricating them as much as he could.

"Such a good boy Allen. Suck it.....oh yeah."

Allen blew out a breath and started moving his left hand again. Roughly pulling and twisting his dick, making it harder, he imagined Frances paying special attention to his erection, making sure he was so hard he was begging for more.

"That's it…get all hard for me. I want to see your dick filling with blood all just for me. All mine Allen all mine…"

Allen closed his eyes, imagining Frances's fingers slowly working him, getting him ready to fuck her brains out.

"Fu-cck…" Allen stuttered wincing as both fingers got to work on his sore dick. His left hand now erratically setting it's own pace making his eyes cloud over with lust and want.

"That's it, fuck my fingers Allen. I want to see you go crazy for me baby boy," she'd say or whatever nonsense words, he wasn't paying attention.

Allen slowly started to pull on and off his two fingers imagining Frances's fingers there and feeling how soft they were. Enjoying how her soft fingers caught on his skin and rubbed some. Closing his eyes, Allen tried to picture what Frances would look like. How her green eyes would darken with desired want…how her dusky, moist lips would catch in the light, making them shine.

Her breath would ghost Allen's mouth as she reached in for a kiss, using her fingers to caress him harder and faster, hitting Allen's sweet spot. Allen jerked in surprise as his fingers rubbed over his sensitive tip.

"Frances….." Allen moaned in wonder, his hand stopping for a brief moment to let his fingers do all the work.

"Alright Allen are you ready to fuck me? Fuck I know you're dying for it. Want to fill me so full and so deep," imaginary Frances said.

Allen's dick was pulsing with need and want. Telling him he wouldn't be able to hang on much longer. He imagined he was penetrating Frances, how she would start grinding slow against him but then increase her pace. He could see Frances all sweaty and beautiful, her muscles bunching and rippling when he slammed into her.

"Fuuccck Frances! So good and tight" he knew she was.

Allen's eyes widened, and his breath came out in shallow

pants. He gripped his now fully hard cock and started twisting again keeping his hips still even as they wanted to jerk, his breath burning his throat. He hurried his pace rubbing faster and faster. He bit his lip almost bloody, trying to hold in the moans that wanted to escape.

"Come for me Allen. Let go, I want to see you come for me," imaginary her said all sultry and hot. With a whimper of Frances's name, Allen came hard and fast. It splattered his hand and on his stomach. He milked himself through the aftershocks, his hand paying special attention to the meaty head. Fuck he would be feeling that for awhile.

*****

"Good morning," Frances said as she padded miserably into the kitchen after throwing up, "How did you sleep?"

"Good. You?" Allen replied drinking his coffee, eyes on the newspaper in his hands.

"Great," she said inspecting the table. There was a variety of things to choose from; toast, eggs, bacon, cheese, fruit, cereal…it was a veritable buffet. For some reason though, Frances stomach was still clenched tight after all the throwing up and she didn't think she could keep much down. So she opted for some cornflakes with cold milk, and a hot cup of coffee. Allen studied her over his newspaper, looking worried.

"You okay?" he asked.

"I'm fine. Just still a bit queasy is all," she replied spooning her cereal.

"Okay well…have you taken your pills?" he asked feeling helpless.

Frances shrugged. "I don't really need them. I'm fine. I just… let me get this cereal down to notify my stomach that everything is hunky dory and then I'm sure it'll allow me to eat all the good stuff."

Allen forced a smile at that and went back to his fruit, eating slowly as he pretended not to watch her.

"So Kareem's coming today," he said by way of a conversation opener.

“Yeah, I’m meeting him at the airport later,” Frances said.

“You excited?” he asked wincing internally at the forced conversation. Sometimes he just didn’t know what to say to her.

“Well I feel anticipation,” Frances said introspectively. “But I’m basically half afraid because my head doesn’t remember knowing this person but my book says we’re really tight. I don’t know how I should behave. It's kind of like when I came home from the hospital…but less intense of course.”

Allen put his paper down. “I had no idea you were so stressed at the time,” he said leaning forward in his concern.

“I wasn’t…exactly. It was more like, a lot of questions going around in my head about how I should behave, relate to you… that sort of thing.”

“But…you’re over that now right?” he asked, his eyes intent on hers. she suppressed a shiver at having the full blast of those gray eyes on her.

"Yeah I'm over it," she said, her voice slightly higher than usual. She hoped he didn't notice.

"Good because the thought of you still pussy footing around is exhausting," he said leaning back in his chair.

Frances picked up an apple and threw it at him.

"Hey!" he said shielding his face. "That's domestic violence. I am totally telling."

Frances laughed, "Oh really? Who are you reporting me to?"

Allen shrugged, "Social services."

Frances laughed even louder, "Aww, do you want them to come take you away to foster care?" she teased.

Allen pretended to pout. "If that's what it takes to get away from you," he mumbled sulkily; his eyes lit up though, to see Frances laughing so freely. What with the awkwardness of being familiar strangers and being pregnant with its resultant shenanigans, he'd felt like the frown hardly ever left her face.

Frances snatched up his phone which was sitting on the side board and handed it to him, "Go on then, call 'em," she said challengingly.

Allen ignored her in favor of drinking his coffee.

"Ha! I knew it," Frances said triumphantly dropping the phone back on the side board. "You can't live without me."

Allen glanced at her and smiled. "Yeah. I can't," he said quietly.

Frances stared at him in shock, literally frozen with it, hand suspended in mid-air as she was reaching out for some fruit. He continued to read his paper like he hadn't just said something earth shattering. She unfroze her hand and forced it to continue on its trajectory to the fruit bowl, but inside her ears were buzzing and she felt dizzy. What was the appropriate response to that? She didn't want him to think that she didn't care; although her freezing over like an icicle probably meant that ship had sailed…but she didn't want to react in an over the top way he would think was either contrived or crazy. She took a deep breath.

“Good to know,” she said aiming for a breezy tone before biting into the mango in her hand.

Allen looked up at her. “Yeah?” he asked. His voice sounded, hopeful?

“Yeah,” she said still shooting for casual but she wasn’t sure if she nailed it or not.

“Good,” he said heaving a deep sigh. “So I was thinking that maybe we should start moving toward a more…I mean…I thought we could go on a date,” he stuttered.

“Oh? Like..now? Kareem is coming,” Frances said in surprise.

“Yeah, I mean, I know…I just meant we could make a date. Go out some day soon,” he said peeking at her and then looking back at his paper.

“Yeah okay, I’d like that,” she replied.

“You would?” Allen asked brightening.

“Definitely,” she said with a single nod of her head.

Chapter 7

"Do you know we don't actually go on dates?" Allen said as they waited for Kareem to clear airport security.

"Oh? Why is that?" she asked.

Allen shrugged, "Probably because we were already living together before we started dating?"

"So what? Married people still go on dates…unless I'm remembering that wrong," Frances said.

"Yeah well…we behaved more like friends with benefits; you know? I mean we went on like work gigs; galas, benefits, dinners…but I don't think we ever dressed up and went out for dinner and a movie or whatever."

"Really. So we just what, had lots of sex and conversation?" she asked turning to face him with interest.

"No…I mean…we did go to the movies and we ate out sometimes; but it wasn't like a date, date…you understand what I'm saying?"

"You're saying you never ask me 'Hey Fran, do you want to go to dinner with me?' or something like that right?"

"Yeah…pretty much," he agreed.

"It's cool. The other way sounds way better anyway. We should just continue like that."

"We really can't. You don't know me anymore so you need to do that. People do that by going on dates."

"If you say so," Frances agreed with a shrug.

"Heads up," Allen said and Frances turned to see where he was looking. There were several people coming out of the terminal but Allen seemed to be looking at a tall chocolate complexioned man with long dreadlocks. He was impossibly handsome too; there was no way someone like that would have gone out with someone like her let alone…

The guy lifted her off her feet and threw her in the air.

"Frances!" he cried happily. "It's been too long."

"Whoa," she replied clutching his shoulders to steady herself.

He put her down and then stuck his hand out for Allen to shake. “Allen? Good to see you man,” he said. Allen shook his hand but didn’t return the sentiment. He inclined his head instead, indicating that they should go.

“You hungry?” he asked. “We can stop for coffee before I drop you crazy kids off home and let you catch up.”

“What happened to Miguel?” Kareem asked. Frances was bemused to know that Kareem knew their cook’s name. It brought it all home to her that she was the one who was missing time.

“He’s still around,” Allen told him.

“Okay then, we can get coffee at home right?” Kareem said. Frances thought he was totally taking it for granted that Miguel would be happy to make them anything they wanted. She herself was still getting used to having a cook who would prepare whatever meal she needed. She stayed silent though and followed the two men to the car. Kareem was dressed in skinny jeans that outlined his legs to muscled perfection with a pink shirt half unbuttoned to show his smoothly toned chest. He had a silver chain with a pendant on the end hanging down between the V of his shirt. He looked like someone's well-kept gigolo. What he *didn't* look like was a man transitioning into womanhood. Why such a dreamily handsome man would want to change his sex was beyond her though, so she just got in the car after him and smiled shyly.

"So…have I jogged anything loose by any chance?" he asked.

"Jogged? Oh you mean my memory? No, Sorry," she said.

"No, don't apologize. It's cool," he said with a wave of his hand. Frances nodded because there was nothing else to say. Allen drove them home and left them at the door before driving off to work. Frances ushered Kareem into the apartment a little shyly. She still wasn't used to the fact that this was her home and she was entitled to be here. Kareem walked in very matter of fact, crossed down the hall to the spare room and deposited his bag on the bed as Frances watched from the door. He took off his shoes, finding some sandals to slip into and then crossed the hall to use the bathroom. Clearly, he was very at home here. Frances leaned on the corridor wall watching him carry out his ablutions. When he was finally all freshened up he came up to her and put his arm around her shoulder.

“Come on, let’s go see if Miguel will make us some tea and then you can tell me everything,” he said leading her back up the corridor to the kitchen. Miguel was way ahead of them; the table was already laid out with a second breakfast. It was like they were hobbits or something; constantly eating. Kareem sat down and eyed the food with relish. Frances sat back a little more slowly pulling the coffee toward her and pouring a cup. She passed him the coffee pot and picked up a slice of dry toast. She was pretty sure she could keep that down.

“So…” Kareem said as he piled his plate.

“So…” Frances echoed with a smile.

“Amnesia huh?” Kareem said.

“Yeah,” Frances said sadly. “I got a big giant hole where 2005 to 2015 should be.”

“The doctors say why its only those ten years you lost?” he asked.

Frances sighed. “Well apparently retrograde amnesia works like that. It takes the most recent memories first.”

“Are they going to come back?” Kareem asked. “What do the doctors say?”

“Well according to them, sometimes they come back, sometimes they don’t. Sometimes you wake up and they’re just back; all of them.”

“What are you hoping for?” Kareem asked.

“Fuck knows. You tell me. What should I hope for?” she asked.

Kareem’s brow rose, “Why ask me?”

“Because I think you know whether there is a hot mess waiting for me or happily ever after,” she said.

"Probably something in between. Believe it or not, you didn't give me every single detail about your love life Frannie," he said.

"Nooo!" she said in mock shock.

"Yes," he said blandly drinking his coffee.

"Well anyway, at least I know that the passion was real if how I feel when he massages my toes is anything to go by..." Frances said watching Kareem for his reaction. He smiled.

"Do you guys...you know," he asked avoiding her eyes.

"You know? You mean like have sex?" she asked leaning forward to find his eyes.

"Yeah. I mean since you don't remember him and shit," he said.

"Yeah, no, we don't. We sleep in the same bed though so it's super awkward," she said.

Kareem laughed. "But you want to?" he persisted.

"Hell yeah. But I can't exactly ask him to jump my bones," she said with a sigh.

"Why not?" he asked.

Frances laughed in disbelief, "What do you *mean* why not?"

"I mean…he's your boyfriend, you're having a baby together; you're practically married! So why not ask him?"

Frances opened her mouth and then closed it, she flicked a glance at him and then back down at her plate. "It's difficult to explain," she said at last. "I don't remember him; I don't remember if that's part of our repertoire…and he kind of intimidates me," she confessed.

"Is it the eyes? You always had a thing about his eyes," he said with a wry smile.

"It's the eyes, and the floppy curly hair and the…" Frances spread her arms out, "the muscles and the height…how the hell did we get together? He could have just about anyone he wanted," she sounded totally bewildered.

"Exactly. And he wants you so…own it sister," Kareem said with a click of his fingers.

"Easy for *you* to say…" Frances mumbled.

“It really isn’t but we’ll put that aside for now. How *are* you feeling about the whole pregnancy thing?” he asked putting his cup down.

Frances frowned. “ I don’t know,” she said with a shrug. “Some days I’m just scared to death, other days I’m excited to be growing another human beings; most days I have heartburn at the myriad of ways I could ruin its life….did I just say myriad? My vocabulary is on point these days…” she finished thoughtfully.

Kareem laughed. “It must be hard to live in your head these days huh?”

“It’s a strange landscape in here definitely,” she agreed.

“Well my advice is…don’t shut Allen out; he’s probably the most qualified person to explain you to you,” he said.

“Great. Can he explain why my toes curl when he massages my back or why I feel like crap when he just goes to sleep without trying to persuade me to have sex with him?”

Kareem laughed, “Maybe not but he’d be stoked to hear it.”

“Would he? Or would it just take a super awkward situation into the stratosphere?” she said and then inclined her head. “There I go with the three dollar words again.”

“You *do* have a university education you know,” Kareem pointed out.

“I know; but in my head I’m still a street rat,” she told him with a twist of her lips and wry brow lift.

“Aww darling; you *are* still a street rat; just a highly educated one,” Kareem teased.

Frances punched him lightly on the arm, fixing him with a mock glare. “You know, I see why you and I are friends.”

“I’ll take that as a compliment,” Kareem replied.

“Mmm,” Frances said swinging her head from side to side in a 50/50 gesture. Kareem laughed and then it was his turn to hit her on the arm.

“Come on, lets go catch up on daytime soaps and I can teach you – *again* – how to put on make up,” Kareem said standing up to the living room.

"Speaking of…are you like…becoming female now or…?" Frances took the opening now that he'd provided it.

"Still taking hormones. I'm taking it really slow for my family's sake. They're trying to be supportive but I get that it's hard for them to let go of 'Kareem'," he said.

"Mmm," Frances said non-committally since she had no idea what the correct response was, "What will you call yourself when you change?" she asked.

Kareem smiled, "I don't know; I'm thinking Aaliyah?"

Frances smiled, "Cute."

"You know it," he said relaxing back on the sofa and clicking the remote.

*****

Allen left them to it all afternoon; he didn't appear like he normally did when Frances was home alone. She appreciated the space but at the same time she wanted to see him; it was messed up. He came back in the evening carrying take out.

"Oh, isn't Miguel going to feel the slightest bit offended at you, getting take out?" she asked.

Allen waved a hand, "He's fine. Tuck in, I got your favorite; fried chicken."

Frances looked in the bag. The chicken looked good she had to admit, although she couldn't specifically remember it being her favorite food. There were French fries in the bag as well, some cheeseburgers and soda.

"Wow. I'm pretty sure this is considered food that's not suitable for health-loving Americans," she said plucking out a chicken leg.

"Are you a health-loving American?" he asked. Frances shrugged.

"Apparently not. Besides, I'm pregnant and this chicken is delicious."

"Let me just get some plates for you," Allen said hurrying to the kitchen.

"Thanks," Frances mumbled around the chicken in her mouth.

They spent the rest of the evening re-watching Con Air simply because Frances couldn't remember seeing it but she remembered wanting to. She enjoyed it immensely while Allen and Kareem enjoyed her enjoyment. They stayed up late simply talking and reminiscing about things, Kareem and Allen drinking beer while Frances stuck to milk. The boys played off of each other, telling outlandish stories of their time in college and making Frances laugh. It was the most relaxed she'd been ever since she came home from hospital.

*****

Frances decided to use the gym in the basement two days later; she had known it was there because Allen occasionally came back from it; sweaty and glistening, wiping his forehead and looking sexy as fuck. She'd been meaning to go see what it looked like but had been feeling too timid. Somehow having Kareem around made her more comfortable so she decided to give it a try. She left Kareem and Allen at the breakfast nook, companionably masticating their meals. She was still queasy from her morning puking session so she wasn't quite ready to eat anyway.

*****

"Hey, just so you know; Frances is sexually attracted to you," Kareem said out of the blue.

Allen looked up from his newspaper, "Say what?"

Kareem gave him a look, "You heard me."

Allen stared at him. "If you're trying to tell me something just spit it out", he said, squeezing the newspaper in his fist.

"I'm just saying that it might be a good idea to pay sexual attention to your wife," Kareem replied sipping his coffee slowly.

Allen continued to stab Kareem with his eyes. "She told you that?" he asked leaning toward the other man lips pressed tight together.

Kareem shrugged. "You could say that," he said, eyes on the beauty magazine he was reading.

“Kareem, I need you to be very clear about what you are saying,” Allen said.

Kareem sighed and went so far as to put down his magazine.

“You need to seduce your wife Allen, I don’t know how much more clear I can be.”

Allen continued to stare at him as if chock full of questions he couldn’t ask.

“Okay then,” he said.

“Good,” Kareem replied with a nod, picking up his magazine and turning the page.

Chapter 8

Kareem went upstate New York for a few days to visit with his cousins, leaving Allen and Frances alone. The house seemed to echo with his absence and they realized that they'd been using him as a buffer to make it easier to be around each other. Now they were left to fill in that gap with television and books.

Allen slid into the seat next to Frances with a novel and started reading. It was a romance he'd found on her nightstand which was set just before the French Revolution, and it was… funny. The characters were a lot like Allen and Frances really were with each other. And. Well. Allen squinted at the page and shifted in his chair reading in disbelief.

"I'm not your fucking bitch."

"Really?" Julian's voice is hushed, half-whispered. He grabs a handful of Loretta's hair and pulls her head back. He kisses her, tongue pushing inside Loretta's mouth and fucking her

with it. Loretta moans, and Julian bites at his bottom lip. "How about now?"

Allen side eyed Frances, imagining her reading this shit. He couldn't imagine her agreeing to being manhandled the way Loretta apparently was. It's ... bizarre that she'd be attracted to reading about this kind of sex. Was it a kink she'd never told him about? Like...*all this time*? Allen didn't know what to make of it...except that maybe it was a little bit hot.

Julian has his other hand resting at Loretta's waist, his thumb rubbing her hipbone.

"I'm not going to fuck you," Julian breathes into Loretta's neck, "not even going to touch you till you beg me to."

Maybe more than a little.

"You're an asshole," Loretta manages to get out, her voice strained and she can feel herself dripping with readiness, desperate for Julian's hand, his mouth, anything.

"I could leave you like this, just leave you on the edge and desperate for anyone to touch you. But I wouldn't let them, Loretta. I'd mark you so they knew who you belonged to."

Loretta closes her eyes and she can visualize Julian sucking bruises into her neck, scratching and biting and marking her everywhere and she chokes out, "Please."

Allen bit his lower lip, thinking he shouldn't be getting hard reading this—wondering for a second if Frances would actually enjoy that. The author sure does sell it like Loretta did. And Frances *was* reading this story. He cut a glance at Frances, who had abandoned the laptop she'd been browsing on around the time Allen started reading. She seemed oblivious, eyes glued to the TV screen.

Julian fucks her through it, pushing Loretta down with one hand on the back of her neck and pulling out just in time to come all over her ass and back, marking her.

Allen finished the story and closed the book, placing it prominently on the table between them. His cock wasn't getting any less insistent about needing some attention. Fuck. He's getting turned on by fiction now.

"So you thought that was hot?" Allen asked, voice slightly hoarse.

Frances shrugged not pretending to misunderstand but not looking away from the TV either. "Yeah. Kind of."

Yeah. The 'kind of' that's so much 'yes' that Frances can't even look at Allen right now. Allen considered that for a few seconds, and then pushed up from the settee. He turned to stand between Frances and the TV, so that Allen's the only thing Frances could see. Allen lifted his chin and squinted down at her, fingers riding the curve of her skull, knuckles closing around the strands of hair. "Really?"

"I mean…if you're gonna do it, might as well…you know," Frances managed to make it sound casual, but Allen could see the way her green eyes darkened almost to black, the slight flush rising in her cheeks. Allen had had a couple of beers and he was pretty sure he could roll with this. He's read enough to understand that it's the domination, the surrender but most importantly the trust. This might actually be fun. God knew it was about time…

He yanked Frances's head backwards, forcing her to look up at him, his tongue teasing the swell of her lower lip before he pushed inside, rough, long, dirty licks at the inside of Frances's mouth. Frances started to reach for him but Allen caught both of her hands around the wrists, and shoved her down against the settee, falling on top of her. Frances's was so soft and yielding and ready, while Allen's cock was an insistent throb between his legs. He rocked his hips into Frances and devoured her mouth with bruising kisses, tongue plunging deep. He put a hand on Frances's face, fingers digging into the soft skin above her jaw, thumb on her chin, pulling her mouth open wider. He took his time, licking the inside of her mouth, biting her lips until they're dusky and swollen, while she squirmed underneath him with each flick of Allen's tongue against the raw skin. When he was done there, he closed his teeth around the muscle in her neck and bit down hard, his other hand grabbing her hipbone and holding it against the cushions while Allen rocked into her. She breathed out in guttural surprise, hips inching up, meeting Allen's, her hand closing on the back of his neck. Allen pulled away, growling as he threw her hand back down against the sofa. He rose up on his knees, giving her a level look before he reached down and grabbed the hem of her shirt, peeling it up over her head. He undid the button and zipper on her jeans next, sliding them down past her hips while she watched him, leaning forward over her as he eased her pants past her knees and kicked out of them. His body hovered over hers like a promise, not quite touching her yet—and then he sat back up on his knees, moving around on the settee until he's straddling her face, one knee on either side. He settled back on his haunches against the cushions, back almost touching the arm rest. She's staring upside-down at him with glazed eyes, understanding complicit. Her lips parted, eyes moving to focus on Allen's dick, tongue flashing out with a look of hunger. Allen nudged at her mouth, the head of his cock brushing her lips, leaving behind a smear of pre-come, wet and shiny across the swell. Frances closed her eyes, tilted her head back and opened her mouth, her soft, warm lips clinging around the head. God, Frances opening up for him like that, a strained, eager sound hitting Allen like a shock, hot breath ghosting against sensitive skin. Allen couldn't help a desperate hitch of his hips, shuddering as he sunk another inch into her mouth. Frances's lips tightened, tongue flickering to taste the tip, the barest pull of suction—and that's it. Allen heaved forward with a grunt, falling, grabbing Frances's head, sliding across the sleekness of her tongue as he buried his cock in deep wet, heat. Her mouth sealed around his dick all the way to the base, sucking like a goddamned vacuum, throat working, tongue wriggling. Allen yanked back, gasping out a breath at the pleasure of the sensation and sunk deep again, felt her throat close around him, velvety and tight. He rode her, slow at first, then thrusting with his hips, slipping, sliding, cock hitting the back of her throat, rubbing against every bit of slick softness clenched around him, the sounds she was making vibrating through his dick and driving him fucking crazy.

Frances tilted her head back even further as Allen sped up, hands locked around her head, driving deep and feeling her moan, the sound humming through Allen's whole body. Allen came gripping bone so hard he felt like he was going to rip Frances's skin off, knowing there would be bruises tomorrow. The thought just made him come even harder, Frances twisting her head underneath Allen and sucking, swallowing, and the sensation smashed right through Allen's brain, erasing everything else.

His hips were still twitching, sliding on instinct, stuttering aborted movements as Frances kept sucking him, and drawing out the sensation until Allen felt raw and full with it.

Allen pulled free with a chattering of teeth, hot shivers running up his spine. He settled his hips next to Frances's head, upper body lying across the length of her torso, chest to belly. He sucked two fingers into his mouth and pulled them out dripping, his other hand moving each of Frances's legs up and apart. His fingers traced a circle around her rim, making it glisten before he dropped his head and licked. Frances practically twisted out of her skin at the touch of Allen's tongue, and Allen was still not a hundred percent sure about this, but fuck it, he was here, and winding Frances up even more was exactly what he wanted. He settled the tip of his tongue into the crease, nudging experimentally, and Frances bucked, pushing into Allen's chin. The taste is slightly musky above the familiar salty tang of skin, and Allen stiffened his tongue and pressed deeper. He could feel the ring of muscle close around him, so tight and searing hot and Frances got so crazy that Allen grabbed her by the thighs, held her open and still. It didn't taste like much now that he was inside, and he thrust deeper. He felt Frances quake to the tips of her toes, gasping; and then let his tongue slide out, tip catching and holding just inside the ring of muscle. He held Frances down then, craning his neck for a better angle, and fucked her with short, sharp jabs of his tongue until she was whimpering, hands clawing as they reach for Allen before they fall away again, squeezing fists into the cushions.

Allen finally tugged his tongue free of Frances, tracing a line along the dripping wet gluteal cleft, so ready and needing. Allen sucked on his fingers again until they're glistening, thick droplets clinging to the tip, and pushed both of them inside Frances's body. He watched her body spread open around his fingers, taking him easily, and shoved in all the way to the end. Frances sounded like she was dying when Allen pushes a third finger inside her. He teased and played, fingers crooking against the sweet spot for a while before he spreads them apart as far as he could, Frances's whole body going rigid. He fucked Frances with deep, hard thrusts of his hand, her whole body rising into shivering, sweating knots, spine bowing up from the settee.

“God...Allen, fuck me.”

“Not yet.” Allen twisted his fingers, enjoying the shiver that raced through Frances, the flex of her inner muscles, clinging to him, wet and hot.

“Allen,” Frances gasped in a breathless rush. “Please.”

“Anything else comes out of your mouth besides moaning and I'll stop.”

Frances shut up, and Allen knew what an effort that must be at this point, the way Allen's been teasing her. Allen lowered his chin, getting a finger on her sensitive nub as he licked a thin line along her insides, latching his mouth onto her with a quick twist of his neck, breathing out hard. Frances was moaning and making helpless noises deep in her throat that went straight to Allen's dick. When he was hard again, he curled his fingers inside Frances, letting the tips drag and push against slick muscle all the way out, and tore his mouth from her clitoris.

Frances jerked against the settee, whole body seizing against the sudden lack of sensation, hands scrabbling over Allen's skin. Allen sat up on his knees and grabbed her shoulders, rolling Frances over on her stomach. Allen sat up and did a 180, switching his knees on either side of her head and straddling her, balls brushing against the back of Frances's neck. He pressed his hands against the couch and lifted his knees, settling his shins against Frances's back before he slowly straightened his legs, body sliding down Frances's until he was melded belly to back against her. He angled his hips up, cock head teasing against Frances as he lay his arms on top of hers, thumb and forefinger circling her wrists and holding tight as he put them up over Frances's head, pressing them into the cushion as he thrust with his hips, head falling back as he sank into her like a knife through warm butter, body swallowing him easily, greedily.

"Fuck, Frances." He closed his teeth at the base of her neck, holding as he strained all the way to the end, bodies meeting,

Frances arching into the thrust as much as she could with Allen's weight on top of her. Allen dug his toes into the settee, shoving just a fraction of an inch deeper, and Frances's hands clutched useless and empty against the cushion, muscles and tendons flexing under Allen's palms.

Allen let his teeth slide free of Frances's neck, whispering against her skin. "Fucking dying for it, aren't you?" Allen snaps his hips back, slamming forward before Frances could answer, and the sound Frances made, the way she arched into Allen and spread her legs wider was more than answer enough. But Allen wanted to hear more, cock dragging back slow and driving in with an upward thrust as he hit that spot inside of Frances, squeezing her wrists. He inched up, chin hooking over Frances's shoulder, whispering hot and thick as he seesaws his hips in and out.

"That how you want it, Frances? Like it like this?"

"God... Allen. Fuck... yes," Frances rasps, words tearing from her with an effort as Allen drove into her again.

“Gonna fuck you raw and useless,” Allen promised, growling the words with a vicious thrust. He held on to the bones in her wrists and let his mouth slide back down to cover the knob of bone at the top of her spine, teeth digging grooves into the skin as he curled his stomach in and under, drilling into her. Hard, fast, vicious strokes, so fucking good; Frances’ hips twitching up helplessly from the cushions with every down-stroke.

Allen sucked against the skin between his teeth until he knew the skin was bruised purple with blood and finally tugged away, hammering into Frances. “Know what you want, Frances,” he whispers, twisting the angle of his cock as he keeps going, tonguing against the mark on the back of her neck. “Not gonna get it until you ask.”

The words burst from Frances’s lips like a flood, neck pushing into Allen’s mouth. “Please, need to, God, please.”

“Need to what?” Allen demanded, body slamming into Frances so hard that her whole body jolted an inch up the settee.

“Need...” Frances arched, moaning as Allen kept fucking her.

“God ...I.... fucking... hate you...”

“What,” tongue licking a wicked trail up the back of Frances’s neck, “do,” fucking deep and pulling out fast, “you,” fingernails digging into Frances’s wrists, “need?”

“Need... God,” Frances gasped, almost senseless.

“Not God,” Allen growed, fucking her even harder.

“Fuck,” Frances groaned. “You’re... such... an asshole.”

“But I’m the asshole... that’s gonna make you come,” Allen purred with heavy promise, smirking as he ground into Frances.

Allen could feel Frances shudder, muscles rippling and tensing, and then the words pulled from her, desperate and broken. “Fuck, Allen. Touch me. Need to... God... need to come, Allen, please. Please.”

Allen released Frances’s wrist and slid his fist between them. He pushed against Frances’ sensitive nub, hot, flushed skin, slick with wetness. Allen played with it for a second before he pressed his finger down and rubbed at Frances just as hard as he was fucking her. Frances came with the force of a bullet from a gun, shuddering and shivering as Allen's fist was suffused with fluid. Allen's hips stuttered as Frances locked down around his cock, muscles fluttering and squeezing--*oh, fucking Christ*...They both bucked and shivered and shook, bodies working counterpoint rhythm, and Allen locked his teeth at the top of Frances's spine and bit hard. Frances cried out, whole body flexing and coiling against Allen, muscles locking around Allen's dick, and there was a split second where Allen couldn't breathe, couldn't see—and then his nerve endings caught fire, shooting sparks all through him before they exploded, body blotting out everything except the extreme force of pleasure ripping through him.

When he could think again, Frances was spread boneless and shivering underneath him. “Yeah... fuck...Fran. So good,” Allen rasped, hips dragging and pushing to fill Frances slowly as he rode out the last edge. He finally collapsed against Frances, both of them sweaty, hearts beating like a trip hammer, neither of them able to do anything but lie there sticky and fucked out and trying to breathe.

Fuck...that was..that was incredible. Allen wondered if it was going to be like this, from now on. Not that it hadn't been extremely good before; but this new Frances added a new dimension to their sex life; probably unburdened by the baggage of the past, perhaps she was just doing what came most naturally. If that was so, Allen couldn't wait to see what would come next.

He slid out of Frances with a last shiver and pulled himself over onto the settee. He didn't make it far, falling shoulder to shoulder next to Frances, both of them on their stomachs. Allen turned to stare at Frances and saw that she was breathing evenly, in and out; eyes closed. He must have wore her the hell out. He smiled smugly, unable to help himself and got up to go clean himself up before moving them both to the bed and falling asleep with his arms around her.

*****

Frances woke suddenly to a dark room and the feel of a heavy arm lying across her chest. She wasn't sure what was happening for a minute but then it all came back to her…all of it. She shot up, staring wide eyed into the dark and felt Allen shift, murmuring nonsense words in protest of her sudden movement before relaxing again into sleep.

"Fuck," Frances whispered moving his hand away and sliding to the side of the bed to get up. "Fuck fuck fuck," she said hand on her stomach as she crossed to the bathroom to stare in the mirror.

"I'm pregnant?" she asked her reflection in horror. Her reflection didn't reply; just mirrored her expression back at her. "How can I be pregnant? We were using protection…mostly," she continued to speak with her unresponsive reflection.

"Fran? You okay?" Allen's husky voice seemed to be coming closer. For a moment, Frances wanted to hide but then she realized that he knew already…knew and was fine with it. In fact, he'd been exceptional in helping her cope. Frances turned to look at him as he came to a stop at the bathroom door. She stared as if she'd never seen him before. He watched her watching him for a while, eyebrows slowly rising higher and higher.

"Fran? What's going on?" he asked at last.

"I remember," she said hollowly.

He stared at her as if waiting for further clarification, "What?"

"I remember everything," she said slowly as if he was brain damaged and deaf to boot.

"You remember," he repeated looking at her with hope in his eyes. "Who you are?"

Frances nodded her head.

They stared uncomprehendingly at each other for an interminable amount of time.

"Fuck," he said.

"You're telling *me,*" she replied.

Allen opened his mouth and closed it again, unable to find words. Frances smiled at him, and the she began to laugh, which made *him* smile. Pretty soon they were both clutching each other and laughing hysterically. They laughed so hard they had to sit down for a minute and just breath.

“Wow, I needed that,” Allen said.

Frances punched him on the shoulder.

“Ouch! What was that for?” he complained rubbing at his shoulder with a twisted look on his face.

“Everything. You walked out on me you bastard,” she said.

Allen smiled wryly, “So you remember that.”

“Yeah! And what the fuck did you mean by that nonsense about having options or some shit?” she demanded.

“I was just fronting and you know it. I left, drove around a bit, and came right back. Only to find emergency services milling about in my driveway and what looked like a body bag being carted away,” Allen said. Then he punched her on *her* shoulder.

“Ouch,” Frances said rubbing absently at the site. “It wasn’t my fault,” she said sulkily.

“Yeah it never is, is it?” He snapped. Frances threw a sidelong glance his way and then sighed and leaned her head back against the door jamb.

“So we’re pregnant huh?” she said.

Allen laughed, “What is this? Greatest hits of your amnesia or what?”

“Just trying to catch up,” she said with a shrug. Allen turned his head to study her.

“If it means anything I’m glad to see you,” he said.

She rolled her head over to meet his eyes. “You’re sure? Because I kinda got the feeling you were enjoying amnesia me *a lot* just back there,” she said. Allen laughed.

“Amnesia you has some serious sex moves,” he said. She hit him on the arm again.

“Hey you wanna take this down to the gym? We could spar it out,” he said rubbing his arm.

"Ha, as if I'd fall for that one. I'm out of practice and you've been in that gym every day."

Allen shrugged, "It was that or jump your bones. Which one would you have preferred?"

Frances was silent, looking off into the middle distance then she laughed. "Hey what if it was that that brought me back? The sex?"

"That would just be like you to have your memory jogged by sex. You're so weird."

"Jeez, thanks. And you're the guy who's in love with a weirdo so there."

Allen laughed. "Guilty," he said and sighed. "You wanna get some food?"

"You owe me a date dude," she replied.

"Fine. Get dressed, I'm taking you out," he said.

"Yay," Frances said standing up. She staggered a bit; her insides were still mush from the pounding they'd taken earlier and her knees were perceptibly weak. She walked swaying from side to side toward her closet. Behind her Allen pulled himself up.

“You need me to help you?” he asked. Frances didn’t have to be looking at him to know that he was looking smug. She grimaced and kept going.

“I’ll see you at the door,” she said.

Allen was silent behind her and then he murmured something that she didn’t quite hear. It sounded like, “Welcome back.”

Chapter 9

They went to McDonalds because Frances wanted a cheeseburger and she felt that if she were looking for a particular cuisine, she should go to the source. The place was loud and busy but they found a table and spread themselves out.

“So…now what?” Allen asked.

Frances thought about it as she chewed her burger; mostly though, she was enjoying the burst of creamy cheese and minced beef in her mouth.

“I think…we probably have to like go to the hospital and have them check me out or something. And then we really have to talk about this baby we’re having. No half-assing it like you did with Amnesia Me.”

“Babe, what was I supposed to do? I mean, you didn’t recall anything about our situation; how were we even supposed to have a coherent conversation?”

“Sooo, do you actually want to have this baby or not?” she asked.

“I want what you want,” Allen said. Frances was shaking her head even before he finished.

“Nope. No. That’s a cop out. I need an answer,” she said.

Allen looked down at the table, chewing slowly on a French fry. “Fine…babies. Uh…I didn’t think I would be having them so early in life you know? I’m only twenty six. On the other hand, I’m kinda excited about it. I’ve been imagining holding it and loving it and it loving me…it's been…nice.”

“So you’re in love with the fantasy of having a child?” she asked.

“I’m in love with the thought of having some untidy haired punk with a smart mouth giving me a hard time all day every day… wait…I already have that,” he said with a grin.

“Jerk,” she said without emotion. “And you’re not going to cop out, however many jokes you make. Gimme an answer.”

"I can't wait for the baby to get here. I'm curious to know him or her. I want to meet him or her. Is that clear enough for you?"

"So you're on board with the baby wagon?" she pressed.

"Yeah Frances, I'm on board with the baby wagon. I want the baby wagon to come into town and sweep us all away. I want the sleepless nights and the crying and pooping, more crying and suckling twenty four seven…all of it."

"That is so cute. I almost believe you," she said.

Allen looked up at her from beneath his lashes. "I know what you're thinking and I don't blame you. The Allen who walked out the door the day of your accident was a child; a sulky child. But that Allen has had to grow up, step up to the plate, become a responsible adult. If you remember what happened when you were amnesiac, you know that's true. I mean would the old me have slept next to you every night without so much as a whimper of complaint about the fact that we weren't having sex?"

Frances made an impressed face, lifting her eyebrows and making an upside down bow with her lips; she tilted her head to the side considering. “I guess, yeah that was terribly obliging of you. I can’t remember you throwing one tantrum.”

“See!” he fisted his hand in triumph.

“So what now? I get amnesia and all of a sudden you’re a grown up? I feel cheated,” she said.

“Blame yourself for letting me get away with murder all those years. You could have put your foot down, you could have left.”

“And gone where?” she asked.

He shrugged, “I don’t know. Wherever you wanted; hell you survived the streets at an age when most of us would have curled up and died; I’m pretty sure you can do anything you want.”

“Thanks for the vote of confidence,” she said dryly, biting into her burger.

"You don't need it. You have anything you need, to be anyone you want. And you know it. So thank you. Thank you for staying with me and tolerating my shit and standing by me all these years. I appreciate it," he said. Frances forgot to chew her food in surprise.

"Okay," she said finally remembering that her mouth was full and closing it.

"And I want to make this official; before the baby comes. Let's get married," he said.

"Whoa there cowboy! We were just getting used to the fact that you're an adult now. And we haven't even discussed the major issue we were facing when I had my accident."

"I thought the issue was my immaturity?" Allen said looking puzzled.

"It's always about you isn't it?" Frances said in amusement.

"Actually no, the issue was…actually now that I think about it, it *was* how immaturely you were handling my burgeoning success. So you're saying you're okay with me having a life outside of you now?" she asked trailing French fries in the sauce so they were thoroughly soaked and then sucking them into her mouth. Allen was distracted by this but he tried to concentrate.

"I wasn't not okay with you having a life outside of me. I just didn't like how much it took you away from me," he protested.

"Are you over that now? Because I have postponed book tours, and appearances I have to make up for…it's going to be a busy time," she warned.

"I can compromise too. You came with me, you supported me when I was just starting out. I can do the same for you. I'll never be happy with not seeing you, you gotta realize that is not going to change; but I can handle it better than I did. I can be a man about it."

Frances studied him in quiet consideration, "I don't even know who you are anymore."

Allen laughed, “Try going to see the love of your life in the hospital and having her look at you like you’re a total stranger. It changes you.”

“So I see,” she replied.

“Anyway that’s over now right? And you still haven’t answered my question.”

“What question would that be?” Frances asked still making patterns in the tomato sauce with her French fries. Allen leaned back in his chair and stared at her in disbelief. She glanced up at him as the silence stretched between them, puzzled as to why he didn’t answer.

“What?” she asked when she found him staring at her.

He sighed theatrically, getting off his chair and coming around to hers. she watched him in surprise wondering what was up. They hadn’t finished eating. He got down on one knee.

“Frances Elizabeth Hilton, will you marry me?” he asked. The table next to them turned to watch, as did various other people milling about. Frances could feel the heat in her face and imagined how flushed she must be. Getting a proposal inside Mickey D's had *not* been on her bucket list. This was blackmail, pure and simple.

"*Yes*, yes I'll marry you, now get up before the entire restaurant stops to watch us," she whispered frantically. Allen was grinning wickedly as he got up, looking supremely satisfied with himself.

"I don't have a ring on me, but I promise you shall have one by the end of the day," he said. Frances could feel her stomach stirring; getting ready to eject everything she'd just eaten into her lap. She stood up quickly and ran for the ladies, hand over her mouth as her body began to heave. The table beside them was extremely entertained by this behavior, with one of the guys going so far as to pat Allen on the back in commiseration.

She made it to the bathroom without embarrassing herself... more and threw up her food regretfully. She had really enjoyed that cheeseburger and she was sorry to see it go. She washed her hands and face, taking her time about it. She had to go out there and face the entire restaurant in a moment, plus she'd just agreed to marry Allen and her stomach was empty. She didn't really know what issue to focus on at the moment but she was basically miserable. Finally, she emerged to find Allen waiting not two steps away, a bag in his hand. He held it up to her.

"I got you a refill. Take away," he said solving two of her major issues in one go.

She lurched forward, throwing her arms around his neck. "I love you," she said gratefully into his neck.

He laughed, snaking his arm around her waist and leading her out of McDonalds, "You're so easy," he said smugly.

She really didn't feel like she could argue with that.

*****

Allen deposited her on the couch with a blanket and her food, stuck in the Game of Thrones DVD and then disappeared. He didn't tell her where he was going and by the time it occurred to her to ask, he was long gone. She settled back in her blankets, enjoyed her food and watched her movie feeling as contented with the world as it was possible to. Unfortunately, the baby was against junk food on principle it seemed, because pretty soon after demolishing the fries, Frances began to have heart burn. She rubbed at her stomach, trying to get some relief but it didn't help. So she snatched up her phone to call Allen.

"What?" he answered but his voice was indulgent.

"I have heart burn," she said sulkily.

"Aww poor baby. You want me to get you some tums?" he asked.

"Yeah," she replied, cradling the phone and close to tears for some reason. "Thanks," she said swallowing the lump in her throat.

"Hang in there baby, I'll be home soon with them okay. Give you a back rub; would you like that?" he asked.

Frances couldn't help it, the tears were just falling on their own. "Yeah," she said sniffing hard and hoping he wouldn't notice.

"Baby what's wrong? Does it hurt that bad?" he asked making her cry harder. She didn't even know why she was crying.

"Okay, give me twenty minutes I'm coming. Can you hang in there for twenty minutes?" he asked, his voice concerned.

"Y-you d-d-don't ha-have to come b-b-back," she managed to get out, breath hitching as she cried.

"Baby hold on okay. Ten minutes," he said and hung up.

Frances dropped the phone and bawled her eyes out. It was the first time she could remember crying like this…ever. Once she started though, she couldn't seem to stop. The tears were endless and they came from the core of her so that her whole body was wracked with sobs. It was bewildering and scary and she just wanted Allen to be here so he could tell her what the hell was happening. By the time he got back, the sobs were petering off and she was exhausted. He came into the house at a run though, face frantic and clutching a package in his hands.

“Frannie?” he said when he saw her, eyes flying over her face in fear. He came to her and she fell into his arms, tears falling afresh as he held her to him as tight as he could.

“What’s wrong baby?” he asked rubbing his hand up and down her back.

“I d-d-don’t kn-now,” she cried into his shoulder. “I c-c-can’t s-s-stop crying!”

“Shhh,’ he said rubbing at her back and her arms, holding her tighter to him as she completely fell apart. He murmured nonsense words to her and at some point she was pretty sure he was singing nursery rhymes. Eventually though, the crying petered off and left hiccups behind.

“Did you –hic- bring the –hic- tums?” she asked because her stomach was still burning up.

“Yeah,” he replied thrusting the small bag he was still holding into her hands. She opened it and saw a bottle of pills, and then there was another box; a black one, square and velvet underneath that. She extracted the pill bottle, popped it and put a tum in her mouth, all without taking her eyes from the other box. As she chewed on the antacid, she reached in to take out the black velvet box. Allen looked startled to see it in her hand.

“Oh, I forgot that was in there,” he said sheepishly.

She stared from the box to him and then back to the box. He took it gently from her hand and opened it, turning it so she could see what lay inside. It was a unique ring or at least Frances hadn’t seen one like it before. The classic styling was perfect, the taper from the lateral sides to the gem natural and beautiful. The detailing was intricate and carefully done. The emerald was dynamic, going from a piercing, dazzling green, to a deeper, more rich tone depending on the lighting and environment. The rose gold was beautiful and added additional classic beauty to an already gorgeous antique flair. The band width was perfect, with subtle details in the band styling. The ring looked different in shade, as opposed to with sunlight directly on it; it displayed a changing energy that Frances could only marvel at.

"It was my mother's," he said also looking at it. "I had it re-sized so it could fit your hand."

"You did that in the last few hours?" Frances asked in disbelief.

Allen smiled looking shy all of a sudden. "Well actually no, I had it done after we got back from the hospital when the doctor said you were pregnant. I had plans to make it official at some point before the baby came. I was just giving you time to get used to the whole idea of me, and pregnancy and amnesia…" he said and he was *blushing*…Frances could hardly believe it; he never blushed.

"So did me getting my memory back throw a curve ball in those plans or…?" she asked.

"Oh yeah definitely. No need to wait anymore," he said with a small laugh.

“Hmm,” she said and looked at him. He looked back at her and they just stood for a while. Then Frances held out her ring finger and Allen took the ring and slipped it on, all without losing eye contact.

“How does it fit?” he asked.

“Perfect,” she replied not looking at it.

Allen nodded his head, “Good.”

Frances smiled.

Allen took a step closer to her as she did the same and their lips met, softly. The kiss was short, and Allen tried to keep it light, but Frances pressed forward and gave it all she had, trying to say everything with this one action. She drew Allen's bottom lip into her mouth and slid her hand into Allen's hair. Kissed him sweet and hard and pulled away slowly, keeping her eyes shut until she was back where she started, hand slipping back to her sides, heart hammering like she just had a near-death experience. Allen’s eyes were still open and he could see the earnest little crinkles at the edges of Frances closed eyes. He could feel her suck his top lip between her own, and hear it when she let out the tiniest sigh against his mouth, like she was just so fucking happy.

“Well,” he said after a stretch where they both just breathed.

“Well,” Frances agreed.

“How is your stomach doing? Still burning?” he asked.

Frances looked down at her still flat stomach in surprise, she’d completely forgotten all about it. “Huh, I do believe its just fine and dandy,” she said musingly.

“Great. Do you wanna maybe take this action to the bedroom?” he asked with a small side smile.

“Seal the deal, so to speak?” she quipped.

“Yep.”

“Always.”

Allen took her hand and led her to their room. He was gentle with her because he hadn’t forgotten the crying jag earlier and it had scared the hell out of him. He didn’t think he’d ever seen Frances cry before. Not even when they’d almost been arrested that one time when collecting for Karl. The mark hadn't wanted to hand over the cash. He was a new guy and thought he could intimidate a couple of kids by pulling in his pal who he said was a cop. Allen had been terrified but Frances had stood up to him and threatened to break his legs if he didn't stay out of business that wasn't his. Heart hammering like a drumstick, Allen had backed her up and he was already a big guy then. The mark had hemmed and hawed a bit just for appearance sake but he handed over the cash when he saw that the 'kids' weren't backing down. It had been a lesson for Allen, Frances might be small and female but you didn't mess with her because she was tougher than all the big tall men in the room.

Coming home with her after that was what had given him courage to stand up to his uncle. Because he knew she had his back, and she would break his uncle's legs if he tried anything funny ever again. Not that he'd seen her actually break anyone's legs but she had the chutzpah to do it definitely. Allen smiled to himself, wondering why he'd never been afraid she would break *his* legs. God know he deserved it on quite a few occasions.

"What are you smiling at," she asked him as she lay in gleaming sated contentment beside him.

He shrugged the shoulder that wasn't deeply embedded in the mattress, "I was just thinking about that time you threatened to break that mark's legs. Remember? The one who said he'd call the police on us?"

"Oh you mean fat Joey? Yeah he was always full of bluster. Generally harmless though."

"I was scared to death," he confessed.

"Yeah? Well you didn't show it," she said turning over to face him and resting her head on her hands. The cold sharpness of her new ring startled her and she moved her head slightly to look at it.

"I don't think I'm ever going to get used to *this,*" she said.

"What? The ring or the life?" he asked.

"I don't know. Both? I mean I have the last ten years back sure, but sometimes being a street rat seems like the only real reality, you know? The rest is like a cruel dream I'll wake up from one day and find that it wasn't real. I'm back in my bunker, I'm alone and nothing has changed."

Allen reached forward and pinched her arm "I'm real," he said quietly.

"Ouch," Frances replied.

"So is that why you were crying earlier?"

It was Frances turn to shrug. "I don't know why I was crying. It was just…suddenly too much. I think I cried for every time I wanted to cry before in my life you know?"

"You finally felt safe enough to," Allen said completely surprising Frances.

"Hey Dr. Phil where'd you come from?"

Allen laughed, "Or maybe its just pregnancy hormones."

"Oh my God, what are you going to say next? PMS?" she scoffed.

Allen just looked at her. “Listen Frances, I’m gonna be serious for a minute so I need you to brace yourself.” Frances actually held her breath.

“I am sorry if I never made you feel safe enough to express yourself the way you needed to, okay?”

Frances laughed. “Trust you to make this about you,” she said in amusement.

“I’m serious Frannie,” he persisted.

“Yeah I know. It's not that I didn’t feel safe. I promise. Maybe it's just the first time I felt safe *and* my hormones were working overtime,” she dismissed.

“Promise me you won’t wait for the stars to align that way next time. If you wanna cry, then cry. Safe room okay? Always,” Allen said.

“Deal,” Frances replied with a smile. “Can we stop talking about this now please.”

“Sure tough guy, go to sleep,” he said.

Frances face screwed up. “I’m kinda hungry.” Allen laughed out loud but he got up to go scrounge for something to eat.

“Hey you,” Frances said sitting up.

“Yeah?” Allen said.

“Thanks for not judging me,” she said.

Allen turned around to say something but Frances dived back into the blanket, covering her head. “Go on, get food,” she said from inside her cocoon. Allen smiled and went.

*****

Kareem came back two days later. Frances hadn’t told him about her recovery because she wanted to see his face when she said she remembered him; but also she needed to tell him about the wedding and she hadn’t previously been aware that he was still in love with her. She still loved him as a very good friend and did not want to hurt him. She didn’t know how she could tell him without doing that. Still, they’d managed to be friends through at least five years of her and Allen being together so he must have contemplated the possibility of marriage between them. Especially now that she was pregnant. Allen told her that it was in fact Kareem who had told him to make a move on her, so she knew he was at least okay with the idea of their togetherness and with them having sex. It was just a hop skip and jump to 'we're getting married!' she hoped. If it wasn't, then for his own good, she might have to cut him loose and she didn't want that.

"Kareem," she said as she opened the door to him.

"Hey girl," he said stepping forward to give her a one armed hug. "Guess what I have for you."

"Cheeseburger?" she asked; it was fast becoming an obsession.

"Guess again," he said holding out a bag to her.

She took it and peered inside; clothes. She reached in and pulled out a pair of black jeans.

"Biker pregnancy clothes!" Kareem exclaimed excitedly. "They have an elastic waist which will expand with your belly."

Frances smiled; they were going to be alright. "You are the best Kareem, you know that?"

"Of course I do. Now go on, try them on," he said shooing her away.

She went off just to oblige him and came back wearing the jeans. They fit her like a glove and the color was perfect for her complexion. It brought out the brightness of her hair and her complexion.

"You are a genius Kareem," she told him, modeling her outfit.

"Thank you kindly," he replied with a smug smile.

"So anyway, I have some news," she told him.

"Spill," Kareem said settling down on the sofa.

Frances spread her hands out and opened her mouth.

Kareem's eyes shifted to her fingers.

"Oh my God, he proposed," he said staring at her ring.

"Gawd you ruined my announcement," she said putting her hands down.

"Oh my sorry. Okay pretend I know nothing. Go," he said.

“I’m getting married!” she exclaimed.

“Yay!” Kareem replied. “About time he made an honest woman of you.”

Chapter 10

Allen was infected with nostalgia at the thought of getting married; he was looking through pictures of his parents, and all the memorabilia they left behind including the postcards they sent from St. Maarten and some photos that had been rescued from their camera. They were so happy and content and Allen took comfort from the fact that their last memories were obviously happy ones. Frances came into the study, carrying a cup of coffee for him.

“Thought you could use one,” she said.

“Thanks,” he replied absently. “How would you feel about getting married on St. Maarten island?”

“What? Where?” she asked caught wrong-footed.

“I was thinking we could retrace my parents’ steps you know? They went to St. Maarten for their anniversary. I thought we could get married there,” he said still studying the pictures.

“Don’t you think that’s a little bit…morbid?” Frances asked.

“Nah. I mean, sure they died in a horrific plane crash returning from there, and that’s maybe a bad memory for me. But for them, they were happy when they were there. I want to turn that memory around. make it good.”

“Well, when you put it like that, I can hardly refuse can I?” she said sitting on the seat opposite his and sipping her own coffee.

“Hey, it's your wedding too. If you don’t want this we don’t do it,” he said looking up at her.

She put down her cup to look at him, “Let’s do it.”

“Great. So next item on the agenda; who are we inviting?”

“I’m guessing your uncle is not on the list?” she asked.

“Nah. No way,” he replied with a quick head shake. “What about you? You inviting Karl?” he asked with a grin.

“Yeah, sure. When hell freezes over,” she said with an answering smile. She picked up her cup. “So okay that’s who we’re *not* inviting. How about who actually makes it onto the VIP list?”

“I was thinking Kareem?” Allen said.

“Well, obvs,” she said.

“And maybe your agent?” he asked.

“Nope. We don’t know each other like that,” she said.

“Then who?” he asked.

“You know I’ve always been the introvert. Kareem and Miguel are my list,” she said.

“Wow. Okay well, mine is a bit longer. I have my college buddies and some people at the foundation,” he said.

“Yeah, okay that sounds about right. What about your high school buddies. I know you guys still Facebook,” she said.

“Yeah…but they were mostly mean to you so no,” he said.

Frances smiled, “Look at you standing up for me.”

Allen narrowed his eyes. “I always did,” he bit out.

“Okay okay, let’s not get our panties in a twist. Do you want a sandwich? I could use a sandwich. Some steak and tomatoes. With cheese,” she said as she stood up and left the room.

Allen watched her go with a smile on his face.

*****

Logistically, it was a nightmare getting everyone to St. Maarten by the following weekend. But Allen wasn't a billionaire for nothing. He hired the best event managers to make sure everything went as planned. They wanted to keep the wedding as exclusive and out of the public eye as possible so they told only those who were attending and no one else. Frances hadn't yet told her agent that her memory was back, they decided to hold off until after the ceremony just so they didn't have to deal with the fall out till then. Frances knew that if the publishers had their way she would be going non-stop for the next few months but for her sake, Allen's and the baby's she knew that was probably not a good idea. Hiding was a temporary fix though and a more permanent one would have to be found soon.

She and Kareem went shopping for a wedding dress because even though he lived in Vegas, he still knew the best places to shop in New York. It wasn't like she was on a budget; Allen had literally given her a blank check, but that didn't mean she was going to go crazy. To that end, they ended up at the The Bridal Garden which was the only not-for-profit bridal boutique in New York City, with donated designer wedding gowns discounted up to 75% off the original retail price. Most dresses were samples, overstock, and once-worn; a majority of the gowns are donated by designers, stores, and brides. The proceeds obtained benefited education for disadvantaged children. It was right up Frances' street. Kareem had made an appointment so they waited in the foyer for someone to come and attend to them. An attendant came hurrying toward them, smiling with welcome.

"Hi. How are you doing?" she asked and then turned to Kareem and frowned. "Er, I should take you through our rules just so you understand."

"Okay," Frances said already intimidated.

"Each bride is allowed to bring two guests to the consultation. Brides cannot bring men or small children into the boutique," she said with a glance at Kareem before continuing. " We do not allow photographs to be taken of the gowns. Brides are kindly asked to remove their shoes before trying on the gowns. Brides are allowed to bring a maximum of five gowns into the fitting room at one time. We kindly ask that brides hang the gowns that she tried on back in the garment bags, and that they be returned to the correct section in the boutique. Deposits are non-refundable and can only be applied towards the purchase of a gown. All sales are final," she finished, like some kind of automaton.

"Er, Kareem is a transgender individual," Frances said in a small voice. It was helpful that he was wearing a skirt/kilt sort of thing and he had on eye liner and lipstick.

The attendant hesitated, clearly at a loss for what to do about this; then she smiled. "I'm sure it will be fine. Come on this way," she said and led them to the shop .

The second dress that Frances tried was perfect. It had a tight bodice that held up her swelling breasts and then fell to the floor in a cascading A-line skirt. It was simple and elegant and she felt absolutely right in it.

“Found it,” she said emerging from the changing room to show Kareem.

He clapped his hands, “You have the eye my dear. It's perfect.”

“Yeah? You really think so?” she asked looking down at herself.

“I know so. Come on, lets go. Time for shoe shopping!” he said. They paid for the dress and left.

“And no discount stores for this!” Kareem said.

“Yeah of course. New shoes for both of us,” she said hooking her arm in his “I like shopping with you – so fun.”

“That’s cause I’m fabulous,” he replied smiling at her.

They ended up at the Glass Slipper which Frances thought was extremely corny but Kareem said it was thee place to shop. She managed to find some flats that would do just perfect. They were Benjamin Adams and were just bright and sparkly. The were known as The Halle wedding shoe which had an all-over crystal look and flat - 1" heel. The open peep toe and closed pump heel were just great for a steady walk down the aisle. She chose the ivory Duchess silk only but with the crystals covering the fabric. Kareem was disappointed at her flat heel, though not surprised. He himself tried on some heels and came away with two pairs of shoes; Milly as well as Pilar by Badgley Mischka.

They were flying to St. Maarten on Wednesday to make sure arrangements were made and bachelor/bachelorette parties could be had. Now that everything was set, Allen was peculiarly excited and he'd stopped going to work to make sure that everything was ready. Frances had a talk with her publisher to let her know she'd be out of town for the next two weeks and then they were off.

*****

The hotel they were staying at was a five star and they booked the entire floor for the wedding party. Since the party wasn't that large, they didn't fill every room but they were able to have a lot of fun since nobody would be complaining about the noise levels. This meant impromptu gatherings in the hallway to eat junk food and bond. Frances got to know Allen's friends a bit better in those two days and they got to know her too, discovering that she was indeed as cool as Allen was always telling them. They were supposed to get married on the beach and the chaplain who was to conduct the ceremony wanted to meet them prior to the ceremony. Which meant putting on some actual clothes and going to meet up with him at his office. He was a kind man, eager to ensure that they were ready for the responsibility of marriage.

"How long have you known each other?" he asked.

Allen and Frances' eyes met and they smiled.

"Who knows? Like ten years?" Frances said.

"Something like, yeah," Allen agreed.

The chaplain smiled. "That's good. So you know each other well. And why do you want to take this step?" he inquired.

“We’re…having a baby,” Allen said bashfully. “And we want to make it official before the baby arrives.”

“Oh, congratulations,” the chaplain said.

“Thank you,” Frances said.

“But what about love. I have not heard you speak of it,” he said.

Frances and Allen looked at each other again. They reached out simultaneously to link hands.

“That’s because we assumed that was a given,” he said.

“Ah, but you know what they say about assumptions,” the chaplain replied with a smile at their entwined fingers.

“We love each other Pastor Jim, and we are planning to spend the rest of our lives together. We’re each other’s family and now our family is growing. For all intents and purposes, we might as well already be married; but the law requires a certificate from a licensed practitioner to say so; so here we are,” Frances explained with a polite smile. Pastor Jim nodded.

"Well said," he said.

"Thank you. So can we get on with it?" she asked.

"Yes. There are just some forms you need to fill out..." Pastor Jim said passing them over, "And a fee that needs to be paid; check or cash will do," he continued.

"Right on," Allen said taking the forms. "It shall be done."

*****

When they got back to the hotel, they found Kareem teaching Allison, one of Allen's college buddies, how to put on eyeliner the *right* way. They had also arranged a joint bachelor/bachelorette party complete with strippers and burritos. They'd arranged to have the party in one of the empty rooms on their floor to make it easier to limit gatecrashers plus they could get as loud as they pleased without bugging anyone. The male strippers were performing in one room while the females were performing in another. Allen was reluctant to be separated from Frances, mostly because he got a look at the male strippers and they were *buff*.

"Okay, compromise," Frances proposed.

"What?" asked Allen.

"I go to your show, you go to mine," she said.

Allen thought about this for a while. "Okay then," he agreed.

Frances got through his show okay, even when one of the strippers was pressing her boobage into Allen's face and his eyes were glued to them. Not for long though, he knew she was watching. When it came to the main show however and one of the dancers was shaking his junk in Frances' face, Allen came forward to pull him away, shaking his head in negation. He was booed by everyone as they called him a wet blanket and spoil sport and pig but he would not be moved. He grabbed Frances, leading her to the dance floor and gave her a lap dance instead. Frances was perfectly okay with that, and so were all the other females in the room when he began to strip.

"Oh my! Oooohh my," Kareem shouted in his MC voice staring around with wide eyes. "We have a stripper situation happening. The groom is stripping; I repeat, the groom is stripping!"

There was a lot of screaming and not all of it was from the bride. There was also a lot of laughing and envious booing from the guys. It was all in good fun and a good time was had by all.

*****

"We are gathered here today to join these two people in holy matrimony," Pastor Jim announced. Frances was radiant in her A line sweetheart floor length Organza gown and her one inch heel sparkly wedding shoes. She felt like the princess she looked like and Allen was her worthy prince in a white tuxedo with gray bow tie.

"You may say your wedding vows," the Pastor said and Allen and Frances turned to each other.

"I promise to be your lover, companion and friend,

Your partner in parenthood,

Your ally in conflict,

Your greatest fan and your toughest adversary.

Your comrade in adventure,

Your student and your teacher,

Your consolation in disappointment,

Your accomplice in mischief.

This is my sacred vow to you, my equal in all things. All things." Allen said looking into her eyes as Frances grinned back. The small crowd applauded when he was done. Then it was Frances' turn.

"I take you to be my partner for life.

I promise above all else to live in truth with you,

And to communicate fully and fearlessly,

I give you my hand and my heart,

As a sanctuary of warmth and peace,

And pledge my love, devotion, faith and honor,

As I join my life to yours." She said, looking him straight in the eye as he smiled at her.

Pastor Jim nodded, "You have the rings?" he asked.

Kareem stepped forward with the matching platinum wedding bands. The pastor blessed them and then it was time to exchange rings. Pastor Jim said the prayer of blessing and then declared them married.

“You may now kiss the bride,” he said spreading his hands out.

Allen looked at Frances and smiled. He leaned forward and she waited for him to meet her, placing his lips gently over hers, he tasted her lips. She opened for him so he could insert his tongue and she sucked it like she was being paid to do so. His whole body surged forward and he enveloped her in a tight hug as he got down to the serious business of kissing her thoroughly. The congregation screamed in appreciation as she opened for him, putting her arms around his neck and holding on fast. She fingered her hands through his hair, playing with it as he explored her mouth thoroughly. The cat calls became louder and ruder but Allen ignored them as he showed Frances exactly how happy he was to be married to her. He only stopped when it was that or sport a painful boner for the rest of the afternoon. They split apart and their small audience burst into raucous applause with slaps on the back of congratulation for Allen and kisses on the cheek for Frances. The after party was held on the beach, with the hotel catering the affair. Since they weren't that many, everyone sat at a long table as the catering staff brought various courses for their enjoyment. In the middle of lunch, Kareem stood up clicking his fork on a wine glass.

"People, hush. It's time for the best person speech," he said. The table quieted down to listen to him.

"So I've known these two since like the second year of college and everybody knows that Frances and I went out and we totally love each other and we would totally be together if she was a lesbian," he said to laughter from the table and Allen throwing a bun at him.

"Anyway, when I first met Allen, I knew he was in love with my then girlfriend because he looked like he wanted to kill me," he said and people laughed some more as Allen shouted, "I did!"

"But the two of us would not be parted because like I said we totally love each other-

"Boo!" Allen cried.

"And we're the best friends each other have ever had," Kareem finished, sticking out his tongue to Allen.

"That said? I totally wasn't surprised when they hooked up about a minute after we broke up; because Frances and I might be best friends but these two? These two are soul mates. They're better together and that is just the truth," he said with a smile turning to face them. Frances blew him a kiss. Kareem picked up his glass and raised it.

"So let's all have a toast to Allen and Frances; may they have a long and happy life together filled with rainbows and unicorns and the crystal droppings of angels," he said as he lifted his glass and drank. The table drank along with him amid bursts of laughter. Then he began to sing.

“Mississippi in the middle of a dry spell

Jimmy Rogers on the Victrola up high

Mama's dancin' with baby on her shoulder

The sun is settin' like molasses in the sky

The boy could sing, knew how to move, everything

Always wanting more, he'd leave you longing for”

Frances and Allen got up to dance on the sand, singing along with Kareem who had a pleasingly falsetto singing voice. The rest of the table swayed and Patrick, another of Allen’s college friends, began to drum out a beat on the table.

“Black velvet and that little boy's smile

Black velvet with that slow southern style

A new religion that'll bring ya to your knees

Black velvet if you please”

Kareem petered off to general applause.

“Music! Let’s have music,” he declared signaling to the DJ who was set up under a palm tree. He continued the song where Kareem left off before going on to other songs.

Up in Memphis the music's like a heatwave

White lightning, bound to drive you wild

Mama's baby's in the heart of every school girl

"Love me tender" leaves 'em cryin' in the aisle

The way he moved, it was a sin, so sweet and true

Always wanting more, he'd leave you longing for

Black velvet and that little boy's smile

Black velvet with that slow southern style

A new religion that'll bring ya to your knees

Black velvet if you please

Every word of every song that he sang was for you

In a flash he was gone, it happened so soon, what could

You do?

Allen and Frances held each other close and enjoyed the song.

“I haven’t heard this song in ages,” Frances whispered.

“You used to hum it sometimes in the bunker,” Allen said.

Frances pulled back from his embrace to look him in the eye, “You planned this?”

Allen shrugged and smiled, “I thought you might enjoy it.”

“I did. I do…God the things you remember…you really do love me don’t you?” she said in wonder.

“I’ve been trying to tell you that for years,” Allen said pulling her back into his arms.

They danced in silence for a while, enjoying the song and each other. Their friends gradually joined them, filling the beach with joy, laughter and happiness.

“Do you really think we can do this?” Frances whispered in his ear.

“Do what?” he asked.

“Be married responsible adults with a kid,” she said.

Allen pulled back to smile at her. “Hell Fran, you’ve been an adult since you were ten. I think you can ace it. And as long as I have you as an example I don’t see how I can go wrong.”

“You do say the most flattering things,” she said patting him on the shoulder in mock annoyance.

“Trust me it's not flattery, just good old fashioned fact,” he replied before leaning in for a kiss.

“Your belief in me will be the death o’ you, you know that?” she said.

“Yeah you’ve been saying that since like ’04; still hasn’t happened.”

“Give it time,” Frances said.

“Sure thing Sherlock. Now shut up and listen to your song,” he said pulling her into him. She laid her head on his shoulder and closed her eyes.

Every word of every song that he sang was for you

In a flash he was gone, it happened so soon, what could

You do?

www.SaucyRomanceBooks.com/RomanceBooks

Black velvet and that little boy's smile

Black velvet with that slow southern style

A new religion that'll bring ya to your knees

Black velvet if you please

Black velvet and that little boy's smile

Black velvet with that slow southern style

A new religion that'll bring ya to your knees

Black velvet if you please

If you please, if you please, if you please.

The end.

If you enjoyed this ebook and want me to keep writing more, please leave a review of it on the store where you bought it. By doing so you'll allow me more time to write these books for you as they'll get more exposure. So thank you. :)

Get Free Romance eBooks!

Hi there. As a special thank you for buying this book, for a limited time I want to send you some great ebooks completely **free of charge** directly to your email! You can get it by going to this page:

www.saucyromancebooks.com/physical

You can see a the cover of these books on the next page:

ONE LONE COWBOY, ONE WOMAN ON A MISSION...
THE LONE COWBOY
EMILY
ROCHELLE
IF IT'S MEANT TO BE...
Him
KIMBERLY GREENFORD
PLAYERS GONNA PLAY?
SHE'S THE ONE HE WANTS
BUT CAN SHE TRUST HIM?
ONE VAMPIRE. ONE COP. ONE LOVE.
VAMPIRES OF CLEARVIEW
J A FIELDING

www.SaucyRomanceBooks.com/RomanceBooks

These ebooks are so exclusive you can't even buy them.

When you download them I'll also send you updates when new books like this are available.

Again, that link is:

www.saucyromancebooks.com/physical

Now, if you enjoyed the book you just read, please leave a positive review of it where you bought it (e.g. Amazon). It'll help get it out there a lot more and mean I can continue writing these books for you. So thank you. :)

www.SaucyRomanceBooks.com/RomanceBooks

More Books By Cher Etan

If you liked this book, you'll love my other book Marriage Of Convenience (Search 'Marriage Of Convenience Cher Etan' on Amazon now to get it). You can see a preview of that below.

Marriage Of Convenience Preview

Here's a preview of my other book Marriage Of Convenience.

www.SaucyRomanceBooks.com/RomanceBooks

Description:

A complete story with no cliff hanger, brought to you by best selling author Cher Etan.

Jonathon is facing losing it all.

His grandfather has given him an ultimatum:

Marry and be in a stable relationship by the time you're 30, or lose out on your inheritance.

There's just one problem; the women Jonathon has so far associated himself with are less than marriage material, and would probably cause more issues in the long run than they're worth.

So when he 'bumps into' Leila on the way to a benefit she's organizing, he soon decides she's the perfect woman for the deal.

Smart, caring and attractive, and not the kind of woman who would get greedy and take him for all he's worth.

But how will Leila, a woman who's been heartbroken in the past, feel about marrying for convenience?

And when Jonathon's granddad realizes his grandson's marrying a woman of color on an average salary, how will he react?

Find out in this touching romance story by best selling romance author Cher Etan.

Suitable for over 18s only due to sexual scenes so hot you'll need an ice shower.

Preview Of The Story:

Leila followed the wheelchair, in which her mother sat, down to radiology preoccupied with the details of how they were going to get through this. There was some sort of problem with insurance and the term ‘pre-existing condition’ was being bandied about with disconcerting frequency. The cost of this test alone, if not covered was going to wipe out at least a quarter of her savings. She tried to school her delicate features when she saw her mother glance back at her. No doubt she realized the seriousness of their situation but still Leila didn't want her to worry. They'd get through this somehow, the money would be found or insurance would pay. What they would not do was despair.

*****

Her mother retired directly after they came home from the hospital, too tired to even attempt to pretend to keep her eyes open. She had an oxygen mask with her that they'd been given at the hospital for her use. The difficulty she had breathing seemed to get worse with each day. Leila knew she hated it. Raychelle Masters was a vibrant, energetic woman who hadn't let her weak chest stop her from working a day in her life. That was probably why she had to practically collapse at work for her to acknowledge there was a problem. Leila had been called at work by her mother's supervisor and informed that her mother had been rushed to hospital. She had dropped everything and rushed to Emory University Hospital where her mother was. They told her they'd had to resuscitate her because she stopped breathing at some point. It was a miracle she was well enough to come home at the end of the day. Well, not well enough…but she'd refused to be admitted and what with the insurance people playing games, the doctors hadn't insisted too hard.

Leila slumped on the chair and let out a breath, trying not to think too hard. There wasn't much she could do tonight anyway, except make sure her mother got through it. The loud astringent tones of Shenaynay telling her to pick up her damned phone startled her quite badly. She frowned at it, making a mental note to beat her cousin Sheila over the head the next time she saw her. Obviously she'd been tampering with Leila's cell phone again.

She picked it up, seeing it was actually Sheila calling…she hesitated, not having the energy to deal with her drama. Not today.

"What?" she asked as she picked up at last.

"Girl what twisted your knickers today?" Sheila replied.

Leila sighed, she really did not have the time. “What do you want Shay?” she asked.

“Relax, my mama asked me to call to ask how *your* mama is doing. Sorry to disturb you and what not but she insisted.”

Leila took a deep breath; there was suddenly a lump in her throat. She tried to get words out but they couldn’t seem to get past the lump.

“Leila?” Sheila prompted.

Leila tried again to get the words out but the lump was blocking her passage completely.

“Okay then, give me thirty minutes, I’ll be right there,” Sheila said in a completely different tone.

Leila tried to tell her not to be stupid; she had class the next day, it was late – too dangerous for her to be out on the street alone; but again, no words came out. And then it was too late, Sheila had hung up.

There was a knock on the door exactly twenty eight minutes later; Sheila was coming from one street over where she lived with her parents and little brother Peter. She was a decade younger than Leila and in university but seeing as their families were close, they tended to act more like sisters and the age difference was easy to overlook.

“Hey,” Sheila said as soon as Leila opened the door.

Leila opened her mouth to return the greeting but it just opened and closed like she was a baby bird waiting for its mother to put a worm down its throat. Before she knew it, she had collapsed against Sheila, her whole body shaking with repressed sobs; all the time aware her mother was just down the hall. And she slept very lightly.

“Oh, baby,” Sheila said patting her on the back and sides and anywhere else she could reach. “Shhh....shhh,” she said even though Leila wasn't technically making a sound.

Leila raised her head to stare desperately at Sheila. “It's bad,” she whispered. “It's really bad.”

Sheila stared commiseratingly at her but didn't say a word. What was there to say after all? She just rubbed Leila's arms and led her back into the house, closing the door behind her. "Let's get you in the bath," she murmured leading Leila to her room. "Have you eaten? How about I make you a nice chicken salad?" she continued to murmur nonsense words at Leila who was clearly not paying attention anyway. She got her undressed, as she ran the bath with fragrant bath salts. Once the water was nice and hot and nearly overflowing, she led Leila into the bath and sat her down, lighting some scented candles and handing her a book.

"Now just relax and catch up on your reading. I'll be in the kitchen making you some delish food okay?" she said soothingly as she left.

Leila lay back, reading the book cover she'd been handed; "Between Death and Heaven", it said. Leila grimaced…not exactly what she wanted to think about right now. She opened it anyway, to see how bad it was. It began with a sex scene so maybe not as maudlin as she'd thought. She lay back in the bubbles, uncaring if her hair got wet, and lost herself in the story.

*****

The chicken salad was great, but the company was better. She tried to make Sheila go home but she wouldn't hear of it. "My first class is at like…eleven o' clock. I got plenty of time to get home and get to class."

"Yeah, but you don't have to. Really."

"Really. I know," Sheila said with a smile, picking up Leila's phone casually.

"Oh no you don't! I just finished redoing my audio profile so the ringtone goes back to "Keep their heads ringing' so you are not going to fuck that up with your fucking Shaynaynay nonsense," Leila said snatching it back.

"Shaynaynay rocks," Sheila protested.

"Weren't you like two in the nineties? There's no way you even remember the original Martin," Leila said.

“Hey, first of all, I wasn’t two, second of all, I was a precocious child,” Sheila said.

Leila laughed which is what Sheila wanted. They watched a few episodes of the sitcom which Leila had on DVD anyway, laughing at Shaynaynay and Martin’s shenanigans before going to bed. Leila woke up almost every hour to check on her mother so by morning she was still exhausted.

“Maybe you should skip work today,” Sheila proposed bringing her coffee.

“Are you kidding me? We have this huge charity event and guess who’s the chief organizer. There is no way in hell I can miss another day of work without serious repercussions.”

“You know what your problem is Leila?” Sheila said handing her some toast.

“I’m sure you’ll tell me,” Leila’s answer was wry.

“You’re too conscientious,” Sheila said.

“Oh dear, I knew it was something serious like that. What is a girl to do about it?”

“Slack off a little bit.”

“I’ll take it under advisement.”

“There you go with the lawyer speak. You know I’m an Art Major right?”

“I know you pretend not to understand a lot of things,” Leila countered.

Sheila laughed, “Touché.”

*****

Leila arrived at the offices of Venture-GRAD, a non-profit that gave scholarships to high school and college students as well as provided support and encouragement to ensure that as many students as possible finished college. She went straight to the conference room where she was scheduled to meet with vendors who were to participate in the charity event she was organizing. She had three days to pull everything together while worried sick about her mother, but luckily, most of the work was done.

Her assistant came hurrying toward her as she approached the conference room.

“Leila, how are you? How is your mother?”

“She’s ill Martha, do we have the RSVP’s all in?” she asked briskly, not wanting the lump to return to her throat.

“All except ten invitees have confirmed attendance. I’ll be calling up those ten today and making a final push.”

“Good good, Martha. Great. Are my vendors here?” she asked.

“All but one,” Martha said.

Leila lifted a brow in lieu of asking who.

“Mr. Smith called to notify us that he’d be running late,” Martha informed her.

Leila nodded. “Okay that’s fine,” she said walking into the conference room where refreshments sat on the sideboard, every vendor had a cup of coffee in front of them and a folder containing all the materials necessary for the meeting. Martha was incredibly efficient as always.

Leila closed the conference room door and smiled at those present. “Good morning,” she said. “Let’s get to work.”

*****

Jonathon Leary walked onto the plane and nodded at the hostess. She smiled at him as she examined his ticket and then gestured toward the first class cabin. She was a pretty thing, with the obligatory blond tresses curling about her narrow shoulders that tapered to a small waist and an attractive swell of hips. Her smile was professional yet warm, Jonathon was sure he could convert that smile into a more personal version, just for him. Maybe later though, right now he had a hangover and he just wanted to put on his sleeping eye mask and drop off. It was a relatively short flight to Atlanta but still, he’d be grateful for the rest. He’d had a really late night last night, partying with his friends but his mother said he had to attend this charity event. She said it was important. They were auctioning him off as a prize for the night; what with the fact that he *had* to be married within the next six months;

mother thought it would be a good opportunity to scope out some talent. He would be thirty years old in six months and if he wasn't married by then, the party was over. Grandpa Movie Star was gonna take it all away.

Most days Jonathon was tempted to let him; having his life dictated to him by some ornery old man who felt entitled just because he was rich and famous was not really what he felt he was put in this world for. And yeah, that old man had paid for his expensive Harvard education and given him the seed money to start his business…but still.

His mother had told him he could do what he wanted, but they were talking about three billion dollars here; was he going to forfeit that just because it came with a coda that he must be married by thirty? Nothing had been said about a necessity for him to be *faithful* to his marriage after all…or even that it needed to last forever. He could find some nice girl, get her to sign a pre-nup and keep her around for a year or three. Inherit his money and keep it moving. It didn't even have to be tawdry or underhanded; who had the energy for that? No, he was sure he could find someone he could stand to live with peacefully for three years. The fact that he hadn't found her yet didn't mean she didn't exist. The kind of women he ran into in his daily life tended toward bottle blonde, vacuous sharks or frumpy weather beaten and bitter. All of whom would be happy to marry him for his money he knew; he just couldn't do that to himself. Even for three billion dollars and counting. Jonathon sighed, trying to shut his mind down so he could sleep but then he felt a presence hovering over him swathed in floral perfume. He lifted his sleeping mask to peer at whomever it was…the stewardess from the door.

"Hey," he said in an inquiring sort of way.

"Hi. I'm sorry to disturb you but we're about to land and you need to fasten your seat belt," she intoned softly. Jonathon stared at her in shock; hadn't he just sat down not ten minutes ago? He peered at his watch and was surprised to see that almost two hours had passed since he got on the plane.

"Wow. Time sure flies when you're asleep," he commented to the flight attendant. She offered him an empty smile and a pointed glance at his seat belt. Jonathon fastened it and then leaned back, readjusting his sleep mask and closing his eyes. There was still time for a nap.

*****

The foundation had sent a driver to the airport in a black luxury SUV. Jonathon was grateful but he also knew it was his grandfather's way of ensuring he'd arrived on time. It was insulting; Jonathon was a grown man. He could travel to Atlanta and attend a charity event without supervision thanks. Still, he got in the back seat and instructed the driver to take him to the nearest coffee place if he would be so kind.

"We have a Starbucks if that'll do yah," the guy suggested and Jonathon nodded his agreement. That was as good a place as any to start.

*****

Leila needed to check on her mother; she'd called twice that morning and her mother hadn't answered. But her schedule was full to overflowing so she guessed she needed to wait for lunch time to make the dash across town. She usually cycled to work because well, the environment, it was cheaper and it was her only exercise; and she'd come to realize it was a much faster means of getting around than sitting in Atlanta traffic. She figured she'd need an hour to get home and back, unless there was a problem in which case she'd have to take the rest of the day off. With that in mind, she tried to get as much done as possible during the morning hours. As soon as the clock struck one pm though, she was out the door like a shot.

Lunchtime traffic was crazy as expected but Leila had her trusty action bike and she wove in and out of it like a pro. She was just passing Starbucks when it happened; she swerved suddenly to avoid running into an unspecified lump on the road and her tire bumped into the side of a huge black SUV and the impact sent her careening into the side of another car. Before she knew it, the world was spinning and she'd landed on a hard surface with a huge thud. She stared, stupefied at the blue expanse above her, unable to make sense of it. A face appeared above her looking concerned. The lips were moving, possibly he was talking to her.

"…-you alright?" she heard.

Her eyes settled on the face, trying to make the world stop spinning by concentrating on one thing. The man's hands came down to run down her arms and his face went from concerned to worried.

"Miss? Miss?" he kept saying. Leila wondered what it was he was missing.

The man shook her and that jolted her out of her reverie because it *hurt*.

"Ouch! Stop it!" she exclaimed in pain, trying to get away from him and go back to staring at the blue expanse. The man stopped shaking her and instead burrowed his hands beneath her body and lifted her up.

“What are you…? Put me down!” she said trying to swat him away. She lifted her arm and saw to her surprise that her sleeve was reddened. She was bleeding.

“What…?” she said in disbelief.

“I’m taking you to the hospital miss,” the man said manhandling her toward his vehicle.

“What? Wait, no..my bike!” she said.

“I’ll put it in the trunk,” the man replied.

“Is she okay?” another man asked standing beside the car.

“She’s bleeding,” the first man said.

“I’m not bleeding,” Leila protested.

“She speaks!” the second man said with an impudent grin.

Leila regarded him askance and then turned to the first man who seemed to be the more responsible of the two.

“Mister, put me down,” she ordered him in the same voice she used to direct her interns.

“Ma’am, you’re bleeding; you need to go to the hospital,” he replied.

Leila was against this plan. “You can’t make me go anywhere. I need to go home. Now put me down,” she said again her voice higher with stress.

“Okay, okay, but your bike wheel is all twisted, won’t you at least allow us to take you home?” the second impudent man said.

Leila peered down through the arms of the man carrying her and saw her bike laying forlorn and injured by the sidewalk. She made a small sound of distress.

“I’ll pay for repairs of course,” the man carrying her said quickly, seemingly afraid that she’d burst into tears or descend into some other form of feminine display of emotion.

Leila said nothing, just allowed herself to be placed in the back seat. She was beginning to feel pain along her arm and at her right ankle so maybe the men were right and she was injured. She didn’t see how taking a ride from the two strangers who hit her was wise though. They were very insistent however, so she decided to go with it but dug into her pocket and extracted her phone. It seemed to have suffered no ill effects in the accident so she took a picture of her erstwhile rescuers and sent it to Sheila with a text telling her that if she didn't hear from her in two hours she was to take the photos to the police.

"Feel better now?" man number two asked after watching her send the text in amusement. She shot him a glare and ignored his remark, looking down instead to inspect herself. There was a hole in the knee of her black pants and her arm was definitely gashed if not actively bleeding at the moment. Her foot looked fine but it was too early to tell if the pain indicated a sprain or a break. She hoped it was neither, please God, she had a fundraiser to arrange by the day after tomorrow.

"I'm Jonathon Leary," the man sitting beside her with the smug smile said.

"Leila Masters," she replied automatically not looking at him.

"That's my driver Mathews, he's the one who hit you and he's very sorry," Jonathon said.

Leila glanced up and then back down to her arm. Was it possible to get through this journey without talking? She could feel the Jonathon dude's eyes on her and she squirmed uncomfortably. How to ask him to stop staring without causing offense and/or showing fear?

"We don't bite you know?" he said further startling her.

"I'm sure you don't," she replied with a fake smile.

Mathews turned around to look at her, "Where can we take you?"

Leila gave them directions to her house and Mathews nodded and turned around to start the vehicle. He'd deposited her bike in the trunk as promised and now he drew smoothly into the traffic. Jonathon sighed theatrically, prompting Leila to look over at him. He gave her a wry glance.

"I was really hoping to get some coffee at Starbucks," he said regretfully.

Leila almost smiled, “Well I didn’t exactly stop you.”

“Indeed,” Jonathon agreed. “But we can’t exactly throw you under our vehicle and then ask you to please wait while we get our coffee fix of the day now can we?”

Leila shrugged, “I don’t know. Can you?”

Jonathon laughed, looking at her with renewed interest.

“So are you like, a professional biker?” he asked.

“No. I’m a lawyer,” Leila said looking him warningly in the eye.

Jonathon shuddered theatrically.

“Oh oh, are we in trouble or what?” he said waving his hands as if he was afraid.

“Well, I’d watch out if I were you and be on my best behavior,” Leila said tongue in cheek.

Jonathon laughed again, “I definitely like you.”

“Lucky me,” Leila replied wryly.

“Oh you have no idea,” Jonathon said, his eyes full of mystery and speculation.

Leila frowned at him but he just stared impassively back. And then he smiled. That was when Leila knew she was in trouble.

*

Want to read the rest? Search 'Marriage Of Convenience Cher Etan' on Amazon now.

You can also see other related books by myself and other top romance authors at:

CPSIA information can be obtained at www.ICGtesting.com
Printed in the USA
LVOW06s0254020915

452388LV00033B/1647/P